'...mpatient voice came in her ear.'

'You know that I don't want to do it,' she said. 'And I'm asking you to reconsider.'

'*Ochi.* Can't be done. You will do what I want you to do.'

'You're a ruthless man, Xenon Kanellis.'

'Insult me all you like,' he said. 'But my heart will not be swayed by your pleas.'

'You have no heart!'

'Then waste no more of my time with your futile protestations. Give me your answer, Lex—is it yes or no?'

There was a pause while she tried to fight it, but she realised she had no choice. 'Yes,' she breathed reluctantly.

'Good.'

Sharon Kendrick started story-telling at the age of eleven, and has never really stopped. She likes to write fast-paced, feel-good romances with heroes who are so sexy they'll make your toes curl!

Born in west London, she now lives in the beautiful city of Winchester—where she can see the cathedral from her window (but only if she stands on tiptoe). She has two children, Celia and Patrick, and her passions include music, books, cooking and eating—and drifting off into wonderful daydreams while she works out new plots!

Recent titles by the same author:

A WHISPER OF DISGRACE
  (Siciliy's Corretti Dynasty)
A SCANDAL, A SECRET, A BABY
BACK IN THE HEADLINES
  (Scandal in the Spotlight)
A TAINTED BEAUTY

THE GREEK'S MARRIAGE BARGAIN

BY
SHARON KENDRICK

First published in Great Britain 2013
by Mills & Boon, an imprint of Harlequin (UK) Limited.
Harlequin (UK) Limited, Eton House, 18-24 Paradise Road, Richmond, Surrey TW9 1SR

© Sharon Kendrick 2013

ISBN: 978 0 263 90048 4

Harlequin (UK) policy is to use papers that are natural, renewable and recyclable products and made from wood grown in sustainable forests. The logging and manufacturing process conform to the legal environmental regulations of the country of origin.

Printed and bound in Spain
by Blackprint CPI, Barcelona

THE GREEK'S MARRIAGE BARGAIN

CHAPTER ONE

WHY HADN'T SHE been paying attention?

Why hadn't she registered the horribly familiar sound of footsteps on gravel?

If Lexi hadn't been thinking about silver earrings—the type which caught the light when you moved—she might have ignored the sharp ring on the bell. As it was, she was completely distracted when she pulled open the door to see the towering form of her estranged husband standing there, sunlight glinting off his ebony hair.

His stance was fixed and immovable. He seemed to absorb all the light which surrounded him, like a piece of blotting paper drinking up a dark spill of ink.

Lexi's heart contracted with pain. The last time she'd seen him he'd been knotting his tie with fingers which had been trembling with rage. A blue tie, she recalled—which had matched his eyes perfectly.

His gaze licked over her now like a cobalt flame. She got the feeling he was undressing her with that gaze. Was he? Didn't he once tell her that whenever a man looked at a woman he was imagining what it might be like to make love to her? And she had listened to him of course, because Xenon had been the expert when it came to sex and she had not. Her heart began to thump heavily in her chest.

Why was he here?

She wished she'd had time to brush her hair. She wasn't trying to impress him, but even so—a woman still had her pride. She thought he looked shocked. As shocked as she felt—though she suspected his momentary loss of composure was for very different reasons. She knew she looked nothing like the woman he had married. The gilded creature who had gazed up at him from behind a misty veil of tulle was nothing but a distant memory. These days she wore the same clothes as other women. She did the same things as other women. No more couture and fast cars. Her hand strayed up to push an errant strand of hair behind her ear. No more expensive trips to the hair salon either.

While he, of course, looked exactly the same.

Six feet two and eyes of blue. Xenon Kanellis. An olive-skinned powerhouse of a man and a legend in his native Greece. A man with a face of dark and rugged beauty. And a man she had never wanted to see again.

'X-Xenon,' she said, her voice stumbling over a word she hadn't said in a long time.

'Thank heavens for that.' He gave the sardonic smile she knew so well. 'For a moment back then I thought you'd forgotten me.'

Lexi almost laughed because the suggestion was so ludicrous. Forget him? It would be easier to forget her own name. True, he wasn't on her mind 24/7 the way he used to be when they'd first split. Before she had decided to take herself in hand. She'd known she would never recover if she continued to obsess about him. The stern talking-to she'd given herself had carried her through the worst. It got her through those bleak, dark days when she had missed him so much that it had felt as if someone had ripped her heart out and crushed it.

But she had recovered because people always recovered, even if at the time they never thought they would. And she had survived worse things than a marriage which should never have happened in the first place.

'You're not an easy man to forget, Xenon,' she said, and then added as an afterthought, 'More's the pity.'

He laughed then but it sounded strange. Maybe she just wasn't used to the sound of male laughter any more. Or the sight of a man—any man—turning up on the doorstep of her cottage and staring at her with such a disturbing sense of entitlement.

His blue eyes bored into her. 'Aren't you going to invite me in?'

Something about his demeanour was unsettling and Lexi felt a flicker of foreboding. 'Is there any point?'

'You're not even a bit curious to discover why I'm here?' He gaze moved over her shoulder, to glance into the cosy interior of her cottage. 'Why I've driven all the way down from London to this godforsaken little place you've chosen to live in?'

'I imagine it must be for your benefit and yours alone,' she answered. 'And if that's the case, then I'm not interested. I've got nothing to say to you that hasn't already been said.'

'I wouldn't speak too soon if I were you, Lex.'

'Veiled threats won't work, Xenon.' She gave him a tight smile. 'Time after time you've refused to give me a divorce and we seem to have reached a stalemate. So unless you've got the papers with you, it's going to have to be hello and goodbye. I'm sorry if you've had a wasted journey but...'

She began to close the door on him but was stopped by his frankly outrageous action of inserting one soft Italian shoe into the narrowing space. For a moment she actually thought about pushing all her weight against it but Lexi knew there was no point in trying. She was strong for a woman, but he was built like an ox. She remembered the first time he'd picked her up and carried her effortlessly to bed. How she had purred her pleasure out loud. Lexi shuddered at the memory. How could she even have *been* that woman?

'I don't need your strong-arm tactics,' she said.

'Tough.'

His eyes met hers and Lexi knew this was one battle she wasn't going to win. 'Then I suppose you'd better come in,' she said ungraciously. 'Perhaps you'd like to beat your chest like an ape while you're at it?'

'I might,' he agreed. 'I know how much that macho stuff turns you on.'

Don't rise to it, she told herself even though she could tell from the cool smile on his face that he seemed to be *enjoying* this. But then Xenon thrived on battle, didn't he? He liked the frisson and the taste of triumph. That was one of the reasons for his global success and his boardroom victories.

Over his shoulder, she could see his gleaming limousine parked awkwardly at the bottom of the tiny lane. It couldn't have been more in-your-face if it had tried and she hoped none of her neighbours were home. She had tired of the fame which had once been hers and had done her best to leave it all behind. She worked hard at being normal. She'd spent time blending into her local community, trying to prove that she was just like everyone else. The last thing she wanted was for Xenon Kanellis to come along and blow all her efforts with one ostentatious display of wealth. 'You're taking up a lot of space with that gas-guzzling piece of machinery.'

'You want me to ask my driver to move it?' He raised his eyebrows. 'I could send her away for a couple of hours, if you like.'

Stupidly, one word registered above all the others. A word which echoed annoyingly in her head. 'You have a female driver?' she questioned, unprepared for the flash of primitive jealousy which shot through her.

'Why not?' He shrugged. 'Weren't you always telling me that I should practise a little more *equality*?'

'Your idea of equality ended when women got the vote, Xenon. I thought you didn't like female drivers? You went on about my driving often enough.'

'That was different,' he said, shutting the door behind him and giving her a patronising smile. 'You are temperamentally unsuited to being behind the wheel of a car, Lex. Probably because of your *artistic nature*.'

She'd only been in his company for five minutes but already Lexi wanted to tip her head back and scream. But anger was good, she told herself. It kept the adrenalin flowing. It stopped her thinking about the pain of the past. It stopped her from wanting him. And that was the crazy and scary thing. That she still wanted him.

'So why are you here?' she asked. 'To remind me how lucky I am not to have to put up with your sexist attitude any more—or is there something else on the agenda?'

For a moment Xenon didn't answer. Instead, he let his eyes travel over her, slowly acquainting himself with someone he'd once known better than any other woman. But the truth was that he was taken aback by her appearance.

The Lexi he'd met and fallen in love with had been a glossy pop-star. A woman with fame at her fingertips and a world who couldn't get enough of her. *Sexy Lexi* the press used to call her and they hadn't been wrong. Everyone had told him she was the last woman he should have married. That a woman like her was ill suited to a man with such fiercely traditional Greek values. Even when she had abandoned her singing career and tried to play the good wife with varying degrees of success, people had still regarded her with suspicion and subsequent events seemed to have proved them right.

Yet the Lexi who stood before him now was a low-key version of the woman who had turned heads whenever she'd walked down the street. The shiny red hair—her trademark look—had gone. She still wore it long, but now it was back to its natural colour; it hung over one shoulder in a thick plait of strawberry-blonde. Gone were the contact lenses she was always losing and, instead, her silvery-green eyes were accentuated by a pair of dark-rimmed spectacles. He didn't think he'd ever seen her wearing glasses before and they made her look oddly serious and surprisingly sexy. The only jewellery she wore was a pair of silver earrings—heavy twists of metal which caught the light as she moved.

In faded jeans and a plain cotton shirt, her transformation couldn't have been more dramatic and it was hard to reconcile this new sober image with the glittering woman he'd married. But with Lexi, what you saw wasn't necessarily what you got. Of every woman he'd ever known—and there had been quite a few—she had depths like no other. Hidden, mercurial depths which had captivated him from the start.

'You've changed,' he said slowly.

She answered his scrutiny with a shrug, even though she could feel the inevitable sting of wounded pride. Because she had seen that look in his eyes and had known exactly what it meant. She had been judged and found wanting and even if it shouldn't hurt, it did.

If she'd known he was coming she would have put on some make-up and changed out of her old jeans. She might have disagreed with such a plan on principle, but what woman wouldn't have made an effort if she'd

known she was about to come face-to-face with one of
the most desirable men in the world?

'Most people change, Xenon,' she said. 'It's one
of the few certainties in life.' But she thought that, as
usual, *he* had managed to buck the trend, because everything about him seemed exactly the same. The same
thick black hair, which could never quite be tamed, no
matter how expensive his barber. The same effortless
elegance—easy when you had a body of muscular perfection which radiated easy power. He always wore a
suit when he was in England and today was no different. His only concession to the warm summer day had
been to ditch his tie and loosen the top two buttons of
his shirt, but that made him look disturbingly acces-
sible. And he wasn't, she reminded herself. He definitely wasn't.

She fixed him with an inquisitive look, knowing that
she needed to get rid of him and as quickly as possible. 'So are you going to tell me why you're here?' she
said. 'Maybe it's my lucky day and you *have* got those
divorce papers. Or are you still stalling?'

Xenon tensed, her flippant tone reminding him of
the essential differences between them. *Keep reminding yourself of those*, he thought grimly. 'I prefer to
think of it as giving time for the dust to settle rather
than stalling. You know my views on divorce, Lex,' he
said. 'Half the problems in this world can be laid at the
door of broken marriages.'

'But when two people can't live together—what's the
alternative?' she questioned. 'A life of misery with two

people trapped in a relationship which has become a nightmare? Surely the world has moved on from that?'

He ignored that. 'Aren't you going to invite me to sit down?' His gaze flickered around the cluttered room. 'To offer me some coffee and show me a little hospitality? Black mark for you, Lex. Have you forgotten all the things you learnt as my wife? Was all my tuition wasted?'

It was a dig at her background. She knew that. He was attacking her where she was at her most vulnerable—a position from which she could never fight back. But today she wasn't going to take the bait because nobody could help where they came from. The only thing which mattered was the person they had become. And she had become a person who was no longer dazzled by the Greek billionaire's arrogance or impeccable background.

'I certainly haven't forgotten your high-handedness and sense of privilege,' she said coolly. 'But since you're clearly not going anywhere, we might as well do this with a degree of civility. Even if we both know it's only a veneer.'

'Oh, Lex,' he murmured. 'What a cynic you have become.'

'I learnt from the very best,' she retorted, leaving him standing in the middle of her sitting room as she went out into the kitchen to make coffee.

Her fingers were trembling as she boiled the kettle and spooned coffee into a pot. Why had he turned up *now*, when she'd just about got her life back on track?

When she'd seen—if not exactly a light at the end of the tunnel—at least some hint that the world didn't have to stay black and miserable for ever.

It hadn't been easy, going from being a famous pop-star to wife of a global magnate—and then back to relative obscurity again. Sometimes her life seemed to have had more transitions than a quick-change artist. The failure of her marriage had been almost unbearably painful at times, but she had come through it. She had survived.

But now it all came rushing back. The pain and the fear. The look on Xenon's face when he'd finally arrived at the hospital with eyes like stone, when she'd lost her baby. The second pregnancy she had failed to carry. When she'd discovered just how unbearably painful a late miscarriage could be. The memory was so overwhelming that for a moment Lexi had to lean over the sink, sucking in several deep breaths of air until she'd composed herself enough to go back into the sitting room.

She set the tray down. He was sitting in a chair which seemed too small for him and his brooding figure seemed to dominate the room.

'So,' she said, handing him a cup. But she didn't sit down and join him. She didn't want to do anything remotely *intimate* because that was fraught with danger. She perched her bottom on the window sill, thinking that looking down on him from a height might give her something of a psychological advantage.

'So,' he echoed. Pushing aside a pile of brochures

which were piled up on the coffee table, he put his cup down and looked around. 'This is a bit of a fall from grace, isn't it?'

She knew it was stupid to react but, even so, Lexi couldn't stop herself from bristling with indignation. 'This is my home and I love it,' she said. 'At least I can close the door at the end of the day and know that I'll find peace inside.'

'But it is small. Surprisingly small.' He fixed his gaze on two goldfish which were swimming round and round in a bowl. Goldfish? Since when did his wife start keeping fish? He frowned. 'I realise that no alimony has been finalised—'

'And I've told you that I don't *need* your money!'

'Which is clearly not true if you're having to live like this.'

'I like living like this!'

'Do you? Yet you walked away from a life where you had homes all over the world—beautiful homes?'

'They were your homes, Xenon, not mine.'

'And now they tell me you are working as a jewellery designer?'

'*They?*' Lexi raised her eyebrows. 'No need to ask how you found that out. I suppose you hired some private investigator to spy on me.'

'I don't consider finding out a few basic facts about my wife to be "spying",' he answered. 'I'm just intrigued by the life you've chosen. You earned a fortune when you were with the band. What's happened to all the money?'

She sucked in a breath, tempted to tell him to mind his own business. Because it wasn't his business and he had no right delving into it. But Lexi knew how persistent he could be. How he liked the facts to be laid out in front of him. If he wanted to know something he was only going to find out anyway—because when you were a man like Xenon Kanellis, you could find out pretty much anything you pleased.

'A lot of it went on my…family.'

'Ah, yes. Your family.' He picked up his coffee and sipped it, wincing slightly at the weakness of the brew. Her background had added to her general unsuitability as a Kanellis wife. She came from the kind of dysfunctional family which had been completely outside his experience. Her mother had never been married and her three children had been fathered by unknown and absent men. The ramshackle, gypsy-like quality of Lexi's home life had appalled him—but even that had not been strong enough to take the edge off his hunger for her. He had brushed aside suggestions that two people from such differing backgrounds might never find any mutual areas of compatibility and had married her anyway. 'How are they?'

Lexi's eyes narrowed with suspicion because there was an odd note in his voice and it was alarming her. Xenon didn't usually enquire solicitously about her family and he certainly didn't drive nearly two hundred miles in order to do so. In the past she might have asked him why he wanted to know—when she was still in that honeymoon phase of believing that things like that mattered. When all their dreams had been intact and lying ahead of them. But she had moved beyond that phase a long time ago and his opinions were no longer relevant.

'They're okay,' she said.

'Really?'

She met his eyes and gave a sigh of resignation. 'Look, you've obviously got something on your mind—so why not just come out and say it?'

There was a pause. 'I've seen your brother.'

'My brother?' she echoed in alarm, because this could only mean trouble. Hiding her sudden sense of fear, she composed her features into an expression of mild interest. 'Which one?'

'I think you know very well which one. Jason.'

Lexi's heart was now going, thud, thud, thud. Jason. Of course. Jason who had been trouble from the moment he was born. Still she kept the tremble from her voice, trying to make her question sound as indulgent as the question of any caring sister. 'What did he want?'

Xenon put his cup down with a small sound of exasperation, watching as her heavy-lidded eyes suddenly became hooded. 'Let's dispense with the air of innocence, shall we? You're not stupid, Lexi. What do you think he wanted?'

The invisible hand which was clenched around her heart grew even tighter and Lexi knew that the time for pretence had passed. 'Money, I'm guessing,' she said numbly.

'Money!' he agreed. 'That thing he can't do without. The one thing he's never bothered to earn himself throughout his useless, idle life.'

'Please don't insult him.'

'Oh, come on—isn't that taking sisterly loyalty a little too far? Since when did the truth become an insult—or have you spent so long avoiding it that you just don't see it any more? And maybe here's a truth you really should take on board.' His body stilled and his eyes grew watchful. 'Don't you see that giving him everything he wants has helped make him the man he is today?'

Furiously, she shook her head and glared at him. Because how would someone like Xenon ever understand? Xenon who had been born into a world of lavish wealth. He hadn't known what it was like to come home from school to an empty fridge. To have to cut a hole at the top of your shoes because you'd outgrown them.

In Xenon's world there had been relatives—far too many of them in her opinion—and servants, who had all doted on him. He'd never had to go to the police station to bail out his drunken mother and then to lie about it to social services, terrified that the family would be split up if the truth ever emerged. He'd never had to hold a terrified and sobbing child who had woken up from yet another nightmare to discover that the real world could be infinitely worse.

'You don't understand,' she said.

'Oh, I think I do,' he said coldly. 'Jason has found that the well of easy money you've always provided has run dry—so who better to turn to than his wealthy brother-in-law?'

The thudding of her heart increased. 'What does he want money for?'

'Why do you think? To mop up the mess he's made of his life with his gambling addiction.'

Lexi closed her eyes as a terrible sense of inevitability crept over her. She'd tried everything to help Jason with his gambling habit. In the early days she had sat down and talked to him and he had lied through his teeth and told her he'd quit. She'd believed every word he'd said as she'd signed over yet another cheque supposed to help put him back on the straight and narrow. Or maybe she had just wanted to believe it. Later, she had paid for the first of many visits to the rehab clinic—until he was kicked out of the last one for starting up a poker school with his fellow patients.

She opened her eyes to find Xenon studying her. 'I expect that you told him no and sent him away,' she said. 'In fact, I'm rather hoping you did. The last counsellor I spoke to told me that I should "withdraw with love".' She saw the perplexed look on Xenon's face as he heard the term and she remembered how disparaging he'd been about people who had sought professional help for their problems. 'It means you have to stop giving him money and bailing him out. It's supposed to make him take control of his own life.'

'Actually, I didn't send him away.'

'You didn't give him money?' Her voice rose in

alarm. 'That's what's known in the business as "enabling".'

'I don't give a damn what it's known as!' he bit out. 'I'm more concerned with the consequences of his actions.'

Her fear growing by the second, Lexi blinked at him from behind her glasses. 'What are you talking about?'

'I'm talking about the fact that Jason has borrowed money. Lots of it. Against your name—and against mine as it happens, since we are still legally married and the Kanellis connection is like liquid gold.' Resolutely, he ignored the horrified widening of her eyes. 'He has built up the kind of debts which made even my eyes water—and I'm no stranger to large sums of money—'

'How much?' she butted in.

He told her and Lexi blanched because she didn't have that kind of money. Not any more.

'And the kind of people he's borrowed it from tend to get rather…*angry* if they don't get their loans back,' he continued.

Lexi's hand flew to her mouth. She could feel the hot rush of breath against her fingers as Xenon's blue gaze iced into her. 'What are we going to do?'

Xenon nodded as a grim feeling of satisfaction washed over him, because that was the first sensible thing she'd said. *We.* 'It looks like I'm going to have to pay off his debt for him—'

'But—'

'There's no alternative, unless you happen to have the money sitting stashed away. That is, unless you want his pretty face altered out of all recognition?' His eyelashes suddenly narrowed, so that his eyes looked like shards of blue ice. 'These people can be dangerous, you know.'

Lexi knew about danger. She'd grown up surrounded by it. And hadn't that been one of the best things about her sudden fame—that she'd been able to escape from the dark and seedy side of life? The last thing she wanted was for Jason to be catapulted back to that place, where nothing seemed safe. She looked at Xenon's hard features, realising that he was offering to help. 'Thank you.'

'Don't thank me until you've heard what it entails,' he said. 'I'll pay off his debt for him—but this time, he doesn't go back to his old life and repeat the same old pattern. And neither does he go into some fancy clinic where he uses that abundance of Gibson charm to manipulate his counsellors.'

'So what are you proposing he does?' she questioned. 'Apply for a personality transplant?'

'Nothing quite so drastic. My solution is simple. He needs to change. To work his body like a man. To see the sun come up in the morning and put his head on the pillow at night, instead of spending it in the casino, like a zombie.' His eyes bored into her. 'And maybe he *wants* to change because he has agreed to go to work for one my cousins in Greece.'

'Are you serious?'

'On one of the family's vineyards,' he continued.

'Your darling brother has agreed to do some hard, physical labour for the first time in his life.'

She stared at him in disbelief. 'He's agreed?'

'I didn't give him very much choice in the matter,' he snapped. 'It was my condition for bailing him out.'

Lexi felt a worrying see-saw of emotions as she took in what he'd just told her. He could be so hard and indomitable that it was all too easy to forget his streak of kindness.

But he hadn't been kind when she'd most needed him to be, had he? He hadn't been there for her at all when she'd reached out for him. He had pushed her away until there had been nothing but distance left between them any more.

'So…why come here and tell me all this?' she questioned.

He gave a cold, hard smile. 'No ideas, Lex? You think I should bail out your brother just out of the goodness of my heart?'

She met the obdurate look in his eyes and a whisper of fear began to creep over her skin as she realised what lay behind his words. 'You mean…there's a price?'

'There is always a price,' he said softly. 'I would have thought you'd have learned that by now. And the price is that I want you back as my wife.'

Lexi's lips opened as if in slow motion, though no words emerged. She could feel the sudden thunder of her heart and a great rush of unexpected excitement because hadn't some rogue part of her always dreamt of just this moment? That Xenon would come back and tell her he was willing to forgive her for walking out. Willing perhaps to try again.

But even as hope flared inside her with a bright, sharp heat, she forced herself to quash it. Because their marriage could never be saved. She knew that. The past held too much sorrow and there could be no future. They might go through the motions of reconciliation—but now a darkness lay at the heart of what they'd once had. And Xenon would never be able to tolerate it.

'Your wife?' she echoed.

His mouth hardened. 'There's no need to look so horrified,' he said. 'It's purely a short-term measure.'

Lexi only just stopped herself from shuddering at her own foolishness, terrified that he would know the crazy thoughts she'd been entertaining. Did she really think that Xenon would be willing to try again? That a man that proud and powerful would be willing to forget the fact that she'd 'humiliated' him with her desertion.

Blankly, she stared at him. 'But why? Why on earth would you want to resurrect our marriage?'

Xenon watched the way she lifted her shoulders in confusion and the gesture made the fabric of her shirt ride over the generous curve of her breasts. The eyes behind her glasses were the silver-green colour of eucalyptus leaves—only right now they were dark with bewilderment. And suddenly he felt a stab of lust so powerful that he could have pressed her down onto the carpet and made her come alive in his arms.

'My sister is having her baby daughter christened and I want you beside me.'

The impact of his words was like a series of small, sharp knives aimed straight at her heart. It hurt to think of his sister managing to produce the first of the next generation. It shouldn't have done, but it did. For her to have succeeded where she herself had failed so badly somehow seemed to bring it all back again. 'I…I'd heard Kyra was married, of course,' she stumbled. 'And that she was pregnant. It just all seems to have happened so quickly.'

He gave a short laugh. 'It was a whirlwind romance, it's true. But you've been gone two years now, Lex. Or did you imagine that the world would stop turning the moment you walked out of my door?'

Lexi's breath was coming in shallow and rapid little bursts. For a minute she actually felt faint. Concentrate on the facts, she told herself. Try to talk him out of this insanity. 'Why would you want me there when we're divorcing? When my attendance there would only excite gossip and comment?' She fixed him with a look of appeal, as if from one reasonable person to another. 'Surely you don't want that, Xenon?'

'It's not just the christening,' he said and now his voice took on a dark and sombre note. 'My grandmother is ill. In fact, she's very ill and they've brought forward the christening, even if she's not actually well enough to attend.'

Despite everything, Lexi's heart turned over. 'I'm sorry to hear that,' she said. 'I know how much you love your grandmother. But your family won't want me there, Xenon—especially not at such an emotional time. Your mother always thought I was the worst possible wife you could have chosen. You know that. And that kind of feeling could spoil the atmosphere and ruin the day for Kyra. What's it going to be like if I suddenly waltz back to Rhodes on your arm?'

'My family will do what I want them to do,' he stated flatly. 'And I want you there.'

Lexi glared. How could she have forgotten his controlling nature? His desire to make everything in the world happen the way that *he* wanted it to? 'You still haven't answered my question, Xenon. Why me, after everything that's happened? There must be hundreds of women who would make more suitable partners. Your little black book was certainly bursting at the seams before I came along.'

'But you were the only woman I married. And my marriage is the only thing in my life which could be considered a failure.' His eyes were steely now. They gleamed with a determination she recognised only too well. 'I don't like failure—perceived or otherwise—and it will make my grandmother happy to see us together again. She believes in marriage. At the end of her life it will please her to discover that her favourite grandson is back with his wife.'

'But that's…that's *dishonest*.'

'More dishonest than you promising to love and to cherish me, until death us do part? Were you remembering those vows when you walked out and broke them?'

To Lexi, this was nothing but a cold-blooded manipulation of the truth, but she bit back her objections.

What was the point of trying to reason with him when he would tie her up in knots with his clever, educated arguments? She wouldn't go to pieces in front of him. She couldn't afford to. She needed to be strong. 'I won't do it, Xenon,' she said quietly.

'But you don't have a choice. Not if you want to save your brother's skin. I suggest you think about it.' His coffee barely touched, he rose to his feet. 'I'll give you until tomorrow lunchtime to make up your mind.'

She watched him as he walked over to the door and Lexi felt like a person clinging to the edge of a cliff whose fingers were slowly slipping. Suddenly the once solid surface of her life was crumbling away and she was losing her grip.

'And if I don't?'

His smile was as cold as steel. 'Then I throw your brother to the wolves.'

CHAPTER TWO

THE NIGHT SEEMED endless and Lexi spent most of it awake, shivering like someone with a fever although the July air was warm. Her nerves felt shot and when the first pale light of dawn began to appear, she gave up all attempts to sleep and pulled back the curtains to watch the sun rise.

But it was difficult to concentrate on anything—even the explosion of light outside her window, which normally filled her with pleasure. Seeing her estranged husband again had stirred up all kinds of feelings—feelings she'd done her best to suppress after the end to her marriage. She'd felt devastated and bereft when it had failed, even though people had done their best to reassure her. They'd said that was the way everyone felt when a marriage ended and she knew that to some extent that was true. But Lexi's pain had been compounded by the loss of their baby.

The thought of that tiny lost scrap of life was still painful and so she got up and dressed before taking herself outside for a walk. Cutting across the fields at the back of the cottage, she walked towards the sea until she had reached the shoreline. The tide was out and it was early enough to still be deserted—with only a lone dog walker striding across the sands.

Her life had taken so many twists along the way. It hadn't turned out the way she'd expected it to—but then, whose life ever did? She had settled in this beautiful part of Devon, an existence which some might have considered dull—but Lexi revelled in the peace and quiet she'd found here after the high-octane experiences of her past.

But she still had responsibilities, no matter how much she sometimes wished she could shrug them off. She'd been a quasi mother to her two siblings. Jake was in Australia now and seemed to be forging a successful career for himself. But Jason was a different story. She'd been at her wit's end with his ongoing problems. She'd thought—hoped—that the reason she hadn't been able to get hold of him had been because he was sorting himself out. Only it seemed that his problems were much worse than she'd thought.

She bent to pick up a shell as she thought about the possibility that her little brother could be in danger and the solution which Xenon was offering.

There is always a price, he had said in that very Greek way of his. And surely the price was too high. How could she bear to spend time pretending to be his wife when barely an hour in his company had left her wanting to climb the walls?

Yet could she deny her brother this chance because

she didn't have the guts to face the man she'd married? What was she so afraid of?

Him. She was afraid of Xenon and the way he made her feel. She was afraid of the things he made her want. Things she could never give him.

She put the shell in her pocket and headed for home. The breeze had whipped her hair into a wild frizz, but at least her cheeks had gained some colour by the time she got back to the cottage. She tried ringing Jason but as usual his phone was switched off and her imagination began to work overtime, and to scare her.

If she denied him this chance for selfish reasons, then wouldn't she spend her life waiting for the knock on the door? The sombre voices of the police telling her that her baby brother had been found in a ditch somewhere?

She picked up the phone and dialled Xenon's number, only to be told that he was in a meeting. But when she gave her name, the tone of the woman answering seemed to change and there was a click before Xenon himself came on the line.

'Lex?'

Still taken aback by the fact that he'd actually interrupted a meeting to speak to her, Lexi forced herself to respond. 'Yes, it's me.'

'You've made a decision?'

'I have.' She kept her voice low and her answers short—afraid she would betray some kind of emotion if she said too much. And the most stupid emotion of all was the hunger welling up inside her. The terrible aching deep in her heart, which made her long for the love they'd once shared.

Maybe it was because the telephone could sometimes play tricks with you. Speaking to someone without seeing the look in their eyes could make you feel as if nothing awful had ever happened. That you were still the same two people who would meet at the end of the day. Suddenly, it was frighteningly easy to imagine him pulling her into his arms and kissing her. Holding her tightly against his big, strong body as he'd done at the beginning. When for the first time in her life she'd felt *safe*.

She gave a wry smile. She should have known it was too good to be true. What was it that they said? That the honeymoon never lasted. And they were right. Because almost as soon as they had returned from their trip to Rhodes, her husband had given himself over to his real love. The work which defined him and drove him and which had made him one of the world's most successful businessmen.

'I'm waiting, Lex,' came the sound of his impatient voice in her ear.

'You know that I don't want to do it,' she said. 'And I'm asking you to reconsider.'

'*Ochi*. Can't be done. You will do what I want you to do.'

'You're a ruthless man, Xenon Kanellis.'

'Insult me all you like,' he said. 'But my heart will not be swayed by your pleas.'

'You have no heart!'

'Then waste no more of my time with your futile pro-testations. Give me your answer, Lex—is it yes or no?'

There was a pause while she tried to fight it, but she realised she had no choice. 'Yes,' she breathed re-luctantly.

'Good.'

She heard the unmistakeable triumph in his voice. She could imagine him sitting in the chair at his desk, swivelling it around so that he could gaze out at the London skyline. And she could have screamed.

'We need to discuss practicalities,' he was saying.

'I agree.' She drew in a deep breath because this bit was much better done on the phone, away from the cal-culating gleam of his eyes. 'So let's kick off by saying that this is not going to be a real marriage in any sense of the word. Let's call it a masquerade, shall we? The mask I'll wear in public won't come off in private. Do you understand?'

'I think it's a consideration which can be discussed at a future date,' he answered smoothly. 'When can you be here? Tomorrow?'

'Are you out of your mind?' Lexi gripped the tele-phone. 'I can't just pack up and *go*! There are things I need to take care of. It may surprise you to know that I have a life here.'

There was a pause. 'Or a man? An eager lover you can't bear to leave behind?'

Lexi almost laughed at how far he was from the truth. How she would have loved to tell him that, yes, there was a man. Someone who thrilled her whenever he touched her, as Xenon had always thrilled her. But there had been no one else. Sometimes she doubted that there ever would be. 'I'm sure that your spies must have reported back to you that currently there's no man.'

'Currently?' he echoed.

'None of your damned business. One of the perks of being separated is that it means you're free to start dating.'

She heard what sounded like Xenon trying to control his angry breathing and she gave a small smile of satisfaction.

'Don't push me too hard,' he growled. 'What do you need to take care of?'

'Well, there's my goldfish, for a start. There's also my jewellery business. I may work for myself but I still have some commissions which I need to finish. When is…?' The lump which had suddenly risen out of nowhere now lodged itself deep in her throat. 'When is the christening?'

'Next week. I'll send my car for you on Friday and we'll fly out on Saturday. Make sure you're ready at noon,' he said, and cut the connection.

Lexi was left clutching the phone, her hand shaking with rage. He was so *authoritative*. So used to getting what he wanted. He hadn't even given her a chance to tell him that she would drive herself up to London. Or should she just let herself be whisked away in his fancy, chauffeur-driven car—no doubt in a demonstration of how easily he could flex his power?

She drew in a deep breath, knowing that she

shouldn't sweat the small stuff. She was doing this for Jason—and all she had to do was to get through it.

She spent the rest of the week finishing up her commissions and thinking about whether she should make something for Kyra's baby. It would make sense and at least it would guarantee that her gift would be unique.

Her career as a jeweller was building slowly, but surely—though at the moment it was confined mainly to locals, with the occasional holidaymaker. Learning how to make silver jewellery had been one of the best decisions she'd ever made. She'd liked the combination of the practical and the artistic and it still thrilled her every time someone liked one of her designs enough to buy one.

Just last week an old man had ordered a chunky brooch for his wife, to celebrate fifty years of marriage. He obviously enjoyed chatting and started telling Lexi all about his long-ago wedding day. She had felt herself getting emotional as his rheumy old eyes welled up with tears and she thought it made her own marital record of two years seem like a mockery.

Picking up a lump of silver, she thought again about the new baby and, although she always steered clear of designing for infants on the grounds that it was too painful, she set to work. Because she had adored Xenon's little sister and she had felt almost *guilty* that the breakdown of her marriage meant that communication with her had been severed. Somehow this handmade gift for Kyra's firstborn seemed important, and significant. She worked long into the night and most of the next day too, until she had fashioned the small silver charm to her satisfaction.

On Friday, she had only just closed up her workshop and finished packing when Xenon's car arrived. Lexi tried not to be intimidated by the female driver who jumped out of the luxury limousine to open the door for her, but it wasn't easy. The wafer-thin woman who introduced herself as Charlotte certainly made her fitted uniform look sexy. Lexi started wondering if there was anything going on between her and Xenon, until she remembered his strict rule about fraternising with the staff. He'd told her it was an important lesson his father had taught him: that you should never sleep with someone you might one day have to sack.

She pushed the thought away, troubled by how much it bothered her. Because it shouldn't bother her. Xenon could sleep with who he liked. They were separated. They were getting a divorce.

She spent the journey watching as countryside morphed into city and her stomach contracted with apprehension as the car drew up outside the gleaming monolithic tower of the Kanellis headquarters.

She gazed up at the plate-glass-and-steel building, reluctantly remembering the last time she had been here. It had been at some company 'do' when the cracks were already beginning to appear in their marriage.

Xenon had been tired and fractious. He'd been working away—*again*—and had come to the party straight from the airport. He had eyed the close-fitting cocktail dress she'd been wearing with the expression of a hungry lion being offered a piece of raw meat and had then proceeded to accuse her of flirting with another man. As if. He didn't seem to *get* that no other man existed for her. She remembered him being angry in the car afterwards and then she'd been angry right back, complaining that he always made her feel like some sort of object or possession. The simmering silence in which they'd sat had grown ever-more resentful, but that hadn't stopped him from practically ripping off her dress the moment they'd arrived home. Or her doing the same with his trousers…

Her breath already dry in her throat, Lexi reached down for her suitcase, but Charlotte must have been watching from the driver's mirror.

'Don't worry about that, Mrs Kanellis. I'll take care of your case,' she said.

Lexi wondered if it was worth going to the trouble of explaining that she no longer used her married name, but decided not to bother. 'Thanks very much.' She gave the young woman a warm smile. 'You're a great driver.'

But her nerves returned when she went into the building, her footsteps clicking as she made her way across the marbled foyer to the executive lift. Stroking her clammy palms down over her dress, she tried not to feel claustrophobic as she rode up towards Xenon's penthouse office. The smoked mirrors threw back distorted images of her face and the dress she wore seemed to have leeched all the colour from her skin and she suddenly felt terribly *provincial*. It was a long time since she had been somewhere like this, somewhere where you could almost *smell* the scent of money.

Xenon's was a success story which business schools used as a template aimed at people for whom no glass ceiling was too high. Born into a wealthy Greek family, he had assumed control of the Kanellis empire after the sudden death of his father—only to discover that the family finances were failing.

Although prodigiously young, Xenon had been undaunted by the task which lay ahead of him, and the fact that the markets had crashed soon afterwards. He had quickly discovered that he possessed the gifts of financial foresight coupled with nerves of steel. He had seen the need to diversify in order to cope with the changeable economic climate and he had done this while assuming the role as head of his extended Greek family, with all the responsibilities that involved.

Through sheer hard graft and dedication, he had revitalised the family shipping line and then added a chain of luxury shops. A newspaper and publishing house had increased the growing value of his portfolio, and during one economic downturn he had bought the rights of a screenplay written by an unknown student. It had captured the Zeitgeist of the time and *My Crazy Greek Father* had become the surprise global smashhit of the year.

But the film had dug much deeper into the national psyche of Greece than the usual stereotypical jokes about sex before marriage and the benefits of moussaka. It had charted the rich and complex history of a beautiful and often misunderstood country. It had detailed wars and defeat. It had chronicled heartbreak and triumph—and had won a plethora of awards for it, included a much-coveted Oscar. The stardust of Hollywood had still been clinging to Xenon's skin when Lexi had met him, some years later, when she had just embarked on an ill-judged solo career.

She knew that Xenon deserved his success. She knew he had worked hard for it and that he still did. But hadn't his insatiable appetite for even *more* success helped drive a wedge between them? Hadn't his ambition grown so big that it had dominated their lives and left her feeling pushed out and resentful?

She had been unable to be the wife he needed, or provide the heir which his fierce Greek pride had demanded. Xenon had wanted perfection and Lexi was a long way from perfection.

The lift pinged to a halt and she walked into the outer office to find a blonde—another blonde!—she didn't recognise seated behind the large desk. Her predecessor had been there for years and Lexi had liked the middle-aged woman who had acted as gatekeeper to the Greek billionaire. It was a little disconcerting to see this new and rather glamorous incumbent rifling through a pile of papers with her shiny pink nails.

The blonde was looking at her and smiling. 'Mrs Kanellis?'

Once again, the words sounded shockingly wrong. Like waking up and finding you were in someone else's body. Lexi wondered how it would go down if she blurted out that she was not really Mrs Kanellis. That she and her estranged husband hadn't shared a bed in almost two years and that Xenon had steadfastly refused to grant her the divorce she wanted. How would the blonde react to that?

But she said none of these things. Instead, she gave the polite smile which was expected of her even if behind it she was gritting her teeth. 'That's right.'

'Mr Kanellis is expecting you. He said to ask whether you would like anything to drink after your journey.'

Tempted to ask for a mild sedative, Lexi nodded. 'A cup of tea would be great.'

'Tea it is. I'll bring some right in.'

A discreet buzzer sounded on the desk and Lexi watched as the blonde smoothed her hand over her already immaculate hair. And that unconscious gesture told her more than a thousand words ever could, because she'd seen it so many times before. She'd seen it with shop assistants and bar staff, with airline stewardesses and female executives. It was a mixture of adoration and availability and it told her that Xenon could still get women adoring him, without even having to try.

'You can go in now, Mrs Kanellis.'

'Thanks.' Tucking her bag under her arm, Lexi headed for the inner sanctum and walked into Xenon's office, shutting the door behind her.

It was an impressive room. One hundred and eighty degrees of glass overlooked some of the most expensive real estate in the capital. In among the skyscrapers were dotted the roofs of famous monuments, looking so out of scale that they would have seemed more at home in a doll's house.

But Lexi barely noticed the view. Xenon dominated that, just as he dominated everything else around him. He was seated at his desk, surveying her with the stillness of the natural predator. His black hair was tousled, as if he had been running impatient fingers through it. He'd loosened his tie—unless the smooth blonde had been responsible—revealing a glimpse of olive flesh which looked warm and inviting. It was only a little thing, but Lexi hadn't been prepared for it. It was too intimate. It reminded her of too much. She knew that the hair began at the top of his chest and arrowed all the way down to his groin. She knew the way she used to scrape her fingernails through it and the way he used to moan in response. It was a mental picture she would have preferred not to have created and it made her cheeks grow hot.

'Sit down,' he said.

Her legs felt weak and she was glad to sink into the chair opposite his. Beneath the filmy folds of her dress, she pushed her knees together, looking at the various trophies around his office. There was the Oscar carelessly standing next to a set of leather-bound books by the great Greek philosophers. On one of the walls hung the platinum disc awarded for the colossal sales of his film's soundtrack and there were several citations from various business schools. A small sculpture by a former Turner Prize winner stood next to a sofa on which he sometimes catnapped, if he was working all night.

All in all, it was a very impressive room which spoke volumes about its occupant.

'So.' She looked at him with challenge in her eyes. 'Here I am.'

'Here you are,' he agreed slowly.

'Why here?' she questioned. 'I mean, why bring me to your office? So you could work right up to the last possible minute, I suppose. Or to remind me of what a successful man you are?'

'Surely you don't need reminding of that?' he mocked.

'Funnily enough, your achievements aren't the first things I think about, on waking.'

'It's neutral territory,' he said. 'Plus you know that I never like to waste time. Why wait for you at the house, when I could be doing something constructive here?'

She met the hard gleam of his blue eyes. 'So work still rules, does it?' she questioned. 'You're still that man who can never say no to earning an extra dollar even though you've got the kind of wealth which could probably bankroll the economy of a small country.'

For a moment Xenon didn't answer. Instead, he just mused on the fact that nobody had ever spoken to him with quite the same degree of insolence as his wife. He watched as she pressed her beautiful knees together and thought she looked a damned sight more respectable today than when he had turned up announced. No. That was the wrong word. You could never use the word 're-spectable' about a woman he could imagine in various states of undress, every time he looked at her.

Lexi wearing nothing but a thong as she'd walked towards their bed.

Lexi sunbathing topless during their honeymoon.

Lexi connecting with something dark and irresistible deep inside him. Something which had enchanted and infuriated him in equal measure, because she had possessed an indefinable power over him and he had resented that.

The first time he'd seen her, he had wanted to ravish her. He had wanted to blot out the rest of the world, so that it was just her and him. It was as simple and as complicated as that and he could remember the moment as if it were yesterday.

She'd recently broken up from her band to launch herself into a solo career. One of her first gigs had been at a big charity function in Bel Air and Xenon had gone along because he'd been a fan of the charity, not of her. He didn't like trashy women who flaunted their bodies and from what he'd heard and seen of The Lollipops all three women had done exactly that in order to get to the top.

With his current squeeze clinging to his arm, he had walked into the crowded ballroom with his prejudices intact and had seen a woman with bright red hair standing on the stage. He had watched her writhing around in a sequinned mini-skirt and had grown hard. He couldn't ever remember feeling quite so turned on as he'd been by Lexi Gibson. It had been exquisite and captivating and so had she. His date forgotten, he had been bewitched by the pale-faced singer.

It had been more difficult than he would have imagined to facilitate a meeting with her. She'd given him the runaround and he got the feeling that she wasn't playing games. She had refused to return his calls and he had been forced to attend her concerts like some run-of-the-mill fan. He'd sent her enough flowers to open a florist's until she had sent him a short note, requesting that the flowers stop. Intrigued and entranced, he had agreed to her request, but only if she would agree to meet him for a drink first. One lousy drink, that was all it had been—but he hadn't been expecting to come away from it still feeling completely smitten. But now it seemed that the feeling had been mutual...

They'd started dating—but it turned out she didn't trust men. It had taken him three whole months to discover that she was a virgin, by which time his need to possess her had become total and complete.

He felt the sudden beat of heat at his groin because that need had never really gone away, had it? Even in the midst of all their rows, he had still wanted her. He wanted her now.

Shifting a little uncomfortably in his chair, he raised his eyebrows. 'Your journey here was okay?' he questioned.

'As okay as any journey can be when you don't particularly want to take it. And your female driver is superb.'

'Isn't she?' The hint of a smile touched the edges of his mouth. 'What about the goldfish you were so concerned about—how are they?'

She eyed him suspiciously. 'They're all right. They've moved in with one of my neighbours.'

'And should I know their names? Just in case their welfare becomes a matter of overriding concern?'

'Are you being sarcastic?'

'Not at all.' He leaned back in his chair. 'There is so much of your life that is now a mystery to me, Lex. I think it wise to learn as much as possible about my wife before I take her home to Greece. Their names?'

'Bubble,' she said. 'And Squeak.'

He frowned. 'That's a meal you eat in England?'

Lexi nodded. A meal that *he* would certainly never have tasted, that was for sure. Frankly, she was amazed that he was interested. In the past, he would never have bothered to ask for such an inconsequential detail, and even if he had she probably would have skated over it. She'd known that her background appalled him and so she'd always played it down—even if doing so made her feel slightly guilty, as if she'd been ashamed of where she'd come from. As if she'd been denying who she really was.

But there was no point in doing that now. In fact, it might even work in her favour. Wouldn't it make this ordeal easier if she reminded him of the fundamental differences between them? It would certainly make it easier for *her* if he didn't look at her like that—with an expression of desire in his eyes which was making her feel curiously vulnerable.

Forcing herself to concentrate, she nodded. 'That's right. Bubble and Squeak is a traditionally English peasant food,' she said. 'It's made of leftover vegetables—usually cabbage and potatoes—fried up together the next day.'

'I fail to see the connection to goldfish.'

'They're cute names. That's why.' It wasn't the whole story, of course, but she ran her thumb over her handbag before meeting his gaze with a defiant look. 'Look, I haven't come here to talk about my domestic arrangements, or my pets. I've fulfilled my part of the bargain by agreeing to this ridiculous charade of being your "wife", so how about you return the favour? Can I please see my brother before he leaves?'

He leaned back in his chair. 'I'm afraid that won't be possible.'

'Why not? Are you keeping him prisoner?'

'If only life were that simple, Lex.' He ran his thumb reflectively along the edge of his bottom lip. 'Jason is already in mainland Greece, working at one of the Kanellis vineyards. I was afraid that seeing you might make him decide to opt for an easier, softer option. It might have encouraged him to tap you for another loan and we couldn't have that.'

'I told you that I'm no longer in a position to hand out loans,' she said.

His eyes were curious now. 'But don't you miss the money?' he asked. 'I don't mean the funds which were available to you as my wife, but before that. You were a very wealthy woman when we met.'

Lexi met the hard gleam of his eyes. She thought it was a funny question for him to ask now, when at the time he had resented her financial independence. He was one of those men who liked to dominate his woman in every way and that included financial. He'd told her that he preferred to buy her things, rather than having her buy them for herself. He'd said that was the man's role: to protect and provide for his woman. It had been hard for someone like her to accept because she'd never relied on anyone but herself.

'To be honest I don't miss it at all,' she said slowly. 'I felt more like *me* once the bulk of the money was gone.'

'I'm afraid you've lost me now.'

She met the cool question in his eyes. Why not tell him? It wasn't as if it mattered any more. She was no longer that anxious woman who had been terrified he'd stop loving her if he saw through to the dark insecurity which gnawed away deep inside her.

'Frugality is my default mechanism,' she explained. 'That's what I grew up with. What I was used to. When you're dirt poor it's tough, but it has its benefits. It makes you hungry—and hunger was what drove my ambition. It's what made me enter that TV reality show at the age of sixteen, even though everybody said I didn't have a chance of winning. But I did win. I confounded all expectations and got myself a recording contract.'

He opened his mouth to reply but at that moment his assistant tapped on the door and entered the room, depositing a tray of tea on his desk. 'Thank you, Kimberly,' he said.

Kimberly smiled and Lexi watched as she walked

back out of the office with the slightly self-conscious confidence of an attractive woman who was wearing a too-tight dress.

'Has *all* your money gone?' he continued.

'Not all of it, no.' Without being asked or offered, Lexi leaned forward and poured herself some tea and this small element of control helped refocus her thoughts. Adding milk and stirring two heaped tea-spoons of sugar into her cup, she shook her head. 'I have my own house—paid off in full—and enough in-vestments to ensure I never starve. And I'm hoping to grow my jewellery design business so that it becomes a viable source of income.'

Xenon watched as she sat there drinking her tea, with the summer sunshine illuminating her hair so that it tumbled down around her shoulders like a pale water-fall. He thought she looked fragile and intensely femi-nine, yet the spectacles she wore gave her a serious and slightly geeky appearance. This was a new Lexi and he didn't know how to handle her. He gave a bitter smile as he thought about the ashes of his marriage. Maybe he had never known.

He got up from his chair. 'Come on. Let's go,' he said.

She finished her tea and put her cup down. 'Where are we going?'

'Home, of course.' An odd kind of smile lifted his mouth. 'We're going home.'

CHAPTER THREE

IT WAS DISORIENTATING being back in the house where Xenon had once carried her giggling over the threshold. Lexi stood in the high-ceilinged hallway of the beautiful nineteenth century building and felt little beads of sweat pricking at her forehead. She knew Xenon was watching her, just as he'd been watching her during the drive from his office to his home in the classical terrace overlooking Regent's Park. She wondered if he had a clue how weird she found it being here again, after all this time. Did he realise that, behind the smile she'd managed to produce from nowhere, her heart was thudding with pain?

Glancing around the hall, she tried to concentrate on the practical—telling herself that it was only bricks and mortar. But it seemed so much more than that. The air was scented with cinnamon and the walls were hung with beautiful paintings, many of them depicting Greece. There was one with the famous view of the St Nicolas Bay, which could be seen from the terrace of the Kanellis estate in Rhodes. She'd always loved that one.

Silken rugs from the East were strewn over the polished floors and the overriding impression was one of solid wealth and stability. But the décor was as masculine as she remembered and little seemed to have changed since last she'd been there.

Lexi gave a wry smile. This had been their home but it had never really felt like *her* home. Her sometimes brash and streetwise persona had deserted her when it came to soft furnishings and the truth was that she'd been intimidated by what to put in the Grade I listed building. She'd been terrified that her lack of historical knowledge would cause her to make some basic error of taste, which would have everyone laughing at her. That was why she'd never dared put her mark on the house. Why she hadn't bought so much as a single vase when she'd lived here.

'It looks exactly the same,' she observed as she brought her gaze back to rest on his face. 'You haven't done much to it.'

'No.' His expression suddenly became closed.

'Why not?'

'Well, masterminding the Kanellis empire takes up most of my time. You know how it is, Lex.'

'Of course. How could I ever forget something as fundamental as that?' She kept her words as flippant as his. 'My mother was an alcoholic and I married a workaholic. Must be something in me that brings out the obsessive in a person.'

He stiffened, as if her words had shocked him—and maybe they had. 'Why are you saying something like that?'

'Because it's the truth and neither of us have to pretend any more. We both know I was the world's most unsuitable wife for you. I'm just reminding us of one of the reasons why.'

He saw the sudden sharp anxiety on her face and something inside him wanted to wipe it away. 'Stop winding yourself up for no reason,' he said gently. 'Try taking a deep breath and calm down.'

'You think that being back here is contributing to my levels of serenity?'

'I don't think anything could do that when you're so uptight. Come on, let's go and sit down and you can relax.'

Having little choice but to obey, she followed him into the garden room at the back of the house, the one which had always been her favourite. She wondered if he'd done that on purpose—to remind her of all the things she'd lost?

Two green velvet sofas overlooked a garden filled with white flowers. White roses scrambled up a far stone wall and tall white daisies stood behind neat hedges of white lavender. She walked over to the French windows and unlocked them, and a mixture of scents and the sound of birdsong filtered into the room.

It felt unbearably poignant. She used to sit here during her second pregnancy, making plans and knitting minuscule little bootees—even though nobody else she knew ever knitted. While Xenon was away on business she would dream about what it would be like when their baby was born. When, magically, he would let go of his heavy workload and the three of them would go walking in the nearby park, just like a proper family.

She turned back to find Xenon's gaze fixed on her and for a split second she thought she saw a flash of understanding in his eyes. But that was nothing but an illusion. She knew that.

Xenon didn't understand how she'd felt—understanding women wasn't something he had been brought up to do. He had fixed and old-fashioned views about the opposite sex and the way they should be treated. He wasn't intentionally cruel, just thoughtless. Women existed to look pretty and have sex with and produce strapping sons and pretty daughters. But she couldn't even do that bit right, could she?

She realised how quiet the house was; none of the usual staff had appeared offering drinks. There was no smiling Phyllida—his long-serving housekeeper—eager to do her master's bidding. No discreet sounds of food being prepared in the large basement kitchen. They seemed to be completely alone.

'So where is everybody?' she asked. 'Is Phyllida still with you?'

'Indeed she is. Her daughter has married an Englishman, so she has no intention of moving, but I sent her and the rest of the staff over to Rhodes to help prepare for the christening. I thought you might prefer to acclimatise yourself before having to face everyone again.'

'Is that what you call it?' she questioned.

'It might help if you tried to relax a little, instead of

looking like a moth dazzled by bright lights. Pretend they're spotlights instead. You're used to those.'

'Not any more, I'm not!' she retorted.

Slowly, she walked around the room, running her fingers across pieces of furniture as if she were reacquainting herself with them, but in reality moving away from the infinitely more disturbing spotlight of his gaze.

She felt like someone visiting one of those museums where rooms were created to represent different eras. She felt as if she'd stepped back into the past. There was that exquisite bowl from China and a carved piece of African wood, which she remembered from her days as mistress of the house, but the silver gleam of a photoframe was a new addition and contained a photo of a baby. A tiny baby with jet-black hair and a snub button for a nose.

'That's Ianthe,' Xenon was saying. 'My niece.'

Sadness welled up inside her and there didn't seem to be a thing she could do to stop it. She wondered if he had somehow forgotten, or whether he just never stopped to think that their own little boy would be two now. That if things had been different, he might have been running around in that garden—swiping at the tall daisies with a chubby little fist. If he had lived.

But no—Xenon didn't seem to have made that fundamental connection. It didn't seem to have occurred to him that a new Kanellis baby might make her yearn for the babies who would only ever be memories. He had never talked about it at the time. He had closed himself off from her and she had felt as if an invisible wall had slid down between them. Why would he want to talk about it now, when to him it was simply something from the past? A disappointment, yes, but something he would have moved on from with that restless shark-like nature of his.

'She's beautiful,' said Lexi brightly.

'Yes. She is very beautiful.'

But Xenon couldn't help noticing the distracted way she was pushing her fingers through her hair. And some age-old instinct made him want to take her in his arms and stroke away some of the brittleness which was making her hold herself like an unexploded grenade.

He hadn't touched her since she had lost the second baby. She hadn't wanted him to and, if the truth were known, it had seemed somehow *obscene* to touch her intimately after what had happened. He had found it easier to give her the space he'd thought she'd needed and she had seemed to want that, too. Until he'd realised that they'd each been locked in their own, private sadness. That it had made a wedge between them which could not be filled. She had left him soon afterwards and for a long time his anger at her desertion had eclipsed all other feelings. But later they had returned, and when they had…

His determination to get her here had been fuelled by those feelings and for once in his life he hadn't really thought beyond that. He hadn't thought past that first moment of triumph of having her exactly where he wanted her.

But now?

Now he realised that it was more complicated than he had anticipated. He still wanted her, yes—he just hadn't realised quite how much. And deep down, he wondered if it was too late. She was staring at him with a mixture of defiance and wariness, like a small trapped animal—and he wasn't quite sure how to handle her.

'You might want to go and freshen up,' he suggested. 'And decide where you'd like to sleep.'

Their eyes met and Lexi felt the sudden tension between them as he dropped the word into the conversation like a rock into a pool. She forced a smile. The kind she used to use if she was being interviewed and wanted to keep the journalist at a distance. A smile which said *don't you dare come too close.*

'And where are you sleeping these days?' she questioned in a voice so careless she almost convinced herself it was genuine. 'Still in the guest bedroom, or have you moved back into the marital bed?'

Xenon's mouth hardened, her remark making him feel as uncomfortable as no doubt she had intended it should. Would she be surprised to learn that he had never slept in their old bed again? That it had been too full of memories of her. That the fragrance from her skin had still lingered there; the memory of her body beside him too vivid to be tolerated.

He gave the ghost of a smile. 'I'm in the blue room these days. Or should I say, nights.'

'Then I'll have the rose room,' she said, choosing one at the other end of the upstairs corridor. 'That'll be perfect.'

But Lexi was lying, because sleeping at the opposite end of the house wasn't perfect at all. Not when he was standing there full of vibrant life—reminding her of all his dark and golden promise.

He was the only man she had ever loved. The only man she had ever wanted—and that feeling had never gone away. She could feel her sadness being stretched and weakened by a powerful moment of desire. She could feel the soft cloak of intimacy settling around them and she tried to push it away.

'The rose room is all yours. All ready and waiting,' he said sardonically. 'If that's what you want.'

'Of course it's what I want.' Deliberately, she widened her eyes. 'Unless you were labouring under the misapprehension that I was going to fall straight into bed with you?'

'I think I know you well enough to know that instant sex was never going to be a certainty, Lex. Even though right now it's the thing which is uppermost in our minds.'

His frankness shocked her but it also excited her. And that was dangerous. 'It might be on *your* mind—'

'Come on, Lex,' he said softly. 'You're surely not going to deny that you want me, that you aren't standing there wondering what it would be like to kiss me again?'

'I'm not.'

'I don't believe you.'

'Believe what you want. It's no—'

He silenced her by placing a finger over her lips and Lexi felt an instant, trembling response. Her eyes met his with a powerful feeling of recognition and she knew she should have protested. But she didn't. She didn't do a damned thing. Not even when he moved his finger to trace it slowly along the outline of her still-trembling lips.

It had been so long since he had touched her. She'd turned her life around and made the best of what she had but sometimes it just wasn't enough. Outwardly she might look as if she was getting on and being successful, but wasn't the truth that sometimes she felt cold and empty and only half alive?

She could feel the stir of her breath against his finger and he must have felt it, too, because she saw his eyes grow smoky. Another danger sign—because she knew how quickly he could become aroused. She knew how effortlessly he could carry her along on that urgent flare of heat. And then what? her conscience screamed. *Then what?*

She wanted to pull away, but she couldn't. He might as well have turned her into a marble statue. But marble didn't ache, did it? And marble didn't feel this hot flood of desire, which was pulsing inexorably through her body. Lexi closed her eyes, biting back the gasp of longing which was threatening to spring from her lips. What did it say about her, that the tip of his finger edging almost innocently against her mouth could make her want to melt?

'Stop that,' she said indistinctly.

He splayed his hands around the span of her waist in a movement of unthinking possession. His head dipped forward so that she could feel the warmth of his breath on her cheek. 'You don't mean that.'

'I do.'

'Then say it like you do.'

'I don't have to say anything.'

'In that case I might be tempted to take your silence as compliance. Although on second thoughts, I might just admit to being tempted and leave it at that.'

She opened her eyes to see that he was lowering his head towards her and all she could read was the sexual hunger written on his face. There was all the time in the world to stop him but she didn't. Of course she didn't. Even when she said his name, it came out more like a plea than a protest. 'Xenon...I... *Oh.*'

Their lips met in a kiss which was hard and hot and hungry. A kiss which shot right off the scale. She could hear the slam of her heart as he pulled her roughly against him. She could taste the warm mingling of their breaths and suddenly a sob was torn from her throat as she flung her arms around his neck and clung to him, railing against him even while he continued to kiss her.

Her words were muffled against his mouth. 'You bastard. You complete and utter bastard.'

'Call me all the names you like if it makes you feel better,' he groaned. 'But don't deny you want me.'

'No. I. Don't.'

'Yes. You. Do.'

His hand was cupping her breast and she was letting him do that, too. She could feel her nipple peaking against his palm and the rush of blood which engorged it so that it felt weighted and full. But this was wrong. She *knew* it was wrong.

'Xenon.' So why was his name coming out as a sultry moan as she curled her fingernails around his neck?

'Don't fight it, Lex. Just remind yourself how much you've missed this.'

'But we're getting a divorce.'

His answer was to pick her up and carry her over to one of the velvet sofas before lowering her down onto it. The soft pile contrasted with the hardness of the body which was pressing down on top of her and she was unable to hold back her excitement as he removed her glasses and put them carefully on the floor.

He turned back to give her his full attention, pushing her hair back from her face so that he could look at her properly, his blue eyes a blur as they burned into her. She felt exposed. Naked. A warm helplessness flooded through her as he bent his dark head to kiss her again but this time the kiss was charged with purpose.

She let her hands splay over the hard musculature of his back. She revelled in the weight of him; the scent and the taste of him. She felt the jut of his hipbones and the heavy weight of his erection as it pushed against her thighs.

It had been a long time since he had made love to her and, oh, she could tell. Her body felt as if it were on fire and her senses seemed to be sizzling into life in a way she'd forgotten could feel so good. She could feel his hand rucking up her dress and the coolness of the air as it hit her bare knees. An insistent heat began to coil through her as he parted her thighs and the pooling of heat at her feminine core was making her squirm. She wanted him to take off her panties. She wanted him deep inside her. Whispering her hands over his silk-covered torso, she heard him suck in a ragged breath. Dragging her nails over his diamond-hard nipples, she began to circle them over the straining material of his shirt and she could feel *his* helplessness, too.

'Lex,' he groaned.

She thrilled at the husky way he said her name. She lifted her hand up to his head, cradling it against her palm so that she could crush his lips even closer. She could feel the silent, slow entry of his tongue and now it was her turn to groan. She felt all her strength melting away as she reached up to grip his powerful shoulders, encountering the structured lines of his jacket as she did so. And suddenly her eyes fluttered open and she pictured what they must look like. She saw herself as if she'd just floated up to the ceiling and were looking down on the scene below. A man still in his work suit, grappling with his estranged wife on the sofa as if she were a cheap date. Starting to have sex with her right there and then, without any preamble or attempt at wooing.

And she was just lying back and letting him.

She pushed him away and this time he must have sensed that she was engaged in more than provocative play-fight, because he didn't object. His breathing was laboured and his smoky eyes were narrowed as he stared at her.

'What's the matter?'

Lexi struggled to sit up, fury heating her blood as she grabbed her glasses and put them on. She wondered, if she hadn't stopped him, whether he would have simply unzipped himself and impaled her right there on the sofa.

'You really need to ask that?' she breathed.

'I'm not in the mood for riddles,' he said, frustration making him snap the words out.

'It's not a riddle and you're not stupid. Think about it, Xenon. You bring me into your house, knowing that this is an already complicated situation which might require a little consideration on your part. But consideration has never been part of your vocabulary, has it? Even after I expressly told you that this wasn't going to be anything other than a masquerade marriage—you leap on me with all the finesse of a sixteen-year-old boy.'

He watched as she got up from the sofa and began to smooth her dress down, his gaze following her as she went to stand in front of the French windows. The light from the garden highlighted the outline of her long, shapely legs and the strands of hair which had worked themselves free from her plaited hair. He felt the painful twist of lust deep inside him as he glared at her. 'Maybe that's because you make me feel like a sixteen-year-old boy again—with all the corresponding doubts and insecurities.'

'Doubts and insecurities?' She gave a short laugh. 'I don't think so. You were born knowing how to handle a woman.'

'Except perhaps for you,' he said. 'You were my one failure in a long and glittering career.'

Exasperated, she shook her head. 'You see? Even when you're making what might almost pass for an apology, you're turning it into some kind of macho *boast*!'

'I am what I am, Lex.' He shrugged his broad shoulders. 'I am Greek and to be macho is woven into my DNA. I thought that's what you liked. Don't you remember telling me that my mastery turned you on?'

Lexi bit her lip. Yes, she'd said that, and more. Much more. Things which now made her wince. But at the time she had meant them. After years of having to cope and be strong for other people, she had fallen for a man who was just as strong. Someone who was looking out for *her* for a change. For once it had been blissful to let someone else take charge. To let someone else make all the decisions. She just hadn't realised that she needed to keep her own strength and that it was wrong to rely on Xenon's. That once you gave someone else permission to take control of your life, you ended up weak and helpless. So that she seemed to have no reserves left to cope with the misfortune which had befallen them.

'I was younger then,' she said. 'And naïve.'

'And now?'

She reminded herself that she was a grown-up and not some simpering girl. She was a woman who had found her own way in the world. Just because an incompatible marriage had thrown her temporarily off course, that didn't mean she needed to hurl herself straight back into it. And hadn't she made a deal with him? Wasn't she doing this for Jason? For the baby brother who'd had such an unspeakable childhood?

She fiddled with her plait, and shrugged. 'Now I'm just doing the best I can.'

Xenon felt a sudden wave of remorse wash over him because in that moment she seemed as fragile as he'd ever seen her. 'You look tired,' he said.

'I am.' The sudden compassion in his voice disarmed her. She saw the anxiety in his face and some stupid moment of weakness made her want to reach out to him. 'There's no need to look so stricken, Xenon. I was just as complicit as you in what just happened. And I'm not denying that I enjoyed it—I don't think I'd get away with a lie that big.'

His blue eyes burned with intensity. 'So share my bed tonight.'

She shook her head. 'I can't. You know I can't. It would cause too many problems and open up too many wounds. And we can't risk that kind of pain again, for both our sakes.'

His narrowed gaze was thoughtful. 'Then you'd better go upstairs and get some rest,' he said. 'And I'll see you later at dinner.'

She straightened her dress and looked up. 'We're having dinner?'

'Of course we are. We have to eat. Now go,' he repeated roughly, forcing himself to turn away from her. Because her body was sending out a siren song so loud that it was almost deafening him. And he couldn't trust himself not to pull her back in his arms and finish off what they had started.

CHAPTER FOUR

'LEX.'

'Mmm?'

'Wake up.'

Lexi stirred and stretched. She didn't want to wake up. She had been in the middle of a dream—the kind you never wanted to end. A beachy type of dream with warm sand and the sound of the waves swishing against the shore. And there had been a man beside her. A man holding her tightly and kissing her and melting away all the cold sadness which was locked away inside her.

Her eyes fluttered open to find Xenon bending over her, and as his silhouette imprinted itself fuzzily in her line of vision she felt a sinking feeling of resignation. Because he was the man. Of course he was. Even her dreams were dominated by him.

Still a little groggy, she sat up and groped for her glasses and the room shifted into sharp focus as she put them on. She was in the rose room—a sumptuous suite of soft petal shades, with tall windows which overlooked the park. She had never actually slept here before, but it was still filled with memories she'd rather forget. Because she'd made love with her husband on this canopied bed. He'd straddled her over there, on that velvet chair. They'd done it on the carpet, too. In fact, they'd made love in pretty much every room in the house.

And they'd very nearly done it again.

She remembered that brief, erotic encounter on the sofa earlier and she felt the pounding of her heart; the heated rush of blood to her face as she recalled the intimate touch of his hands on her after so long without it. She shouldn't have let it get that far and she shouldn't have shown him how much she still wanted him. But how could she fail to want him when he was so damned gorgeous? When, even now, all she could think about was all the pleasure he had given her in the past and the way she used to choke out his name with disbelieving joy. She needed to remember the pain instead. To protect herself with the memory of how much he had hurt her.

She pushed her mussed hair back from her face and sat up, trying not to focus on the powerful thrust of his thighs, which were distractingly close. 'What time is it?'

'Seven o'clock. You've been asleep for a while.' He studied her rumpled appearance. 'Do you want to get changed for dinner?'

Of course she did, even though the fact that *he* had been the one to suggest it made her want to rebel. He'd grown up in the kind of world where even families changed for dinner and ate formally. The first time she'd met his mother she'd mistakenly thought that, because they were all on a relaxed Greek island, it might be okay for her to wear a denim skirt and a T-shirt to dinner. Big mistake. Her mother-in-law had been decked in silk and pearls, her disapproval freezing the warm Greek air as she had studied the laid-back appearance of her new daughter-in-law.

Lexi glared at him, realising that she was going to be subjected to that level of disapproval all over again. His mother had been frosty enough towards her when they'd been newly-weds. What was her attitude likely to be towards a wife who had left her precious son? 'I'd like to know what the plan is,' she said. 'When are we going to Rhodes?'

'Eager to get there, are you, Lex?' His blue eyes mocked her.

'Not really. But the sooner it's done, then the sooner I can erase this whole ghastly incident from my mind.' She swung her legs over the edge of the bed, wondering if her words carried the lack of conviction she felt inside. Walking over to the dressing table, she picked up a hairbrush. 'I can't believe I'm back in this damned house,' she muttered as she stared at her pinched reflection in the mirror.

'Can't you?' Xenon watched as she began to pull a brush through the tumble of her hair and suddenly he realised he had missed this indefinable intimacy of married life. Watching his wife get dressed—an experience almost as erotic as seeing the whole process later completed in reverse.

He'd missed the shared look which could convey the

meaning of an entire sentence in a single glance. He had missed that easy shorthand more than he'd ever imagined. Perhaps that was why his next words came out in a rush, for he had not planned to say them. 'I thought you might consider giving our marriage another go. Didn't you ever think you might do that, Lex?'

Lexi's hand stilled, mid-stroke. It was an unusually candid question and one she was tempted to brush off with a glib response. But something in the brilliance of his reflected blue gaze melted away her intention. She realised that she mustn't allow pride to skew her judgement. Just because their marriage hadn't worked out, didn't mean that she had to devalue it completely, did it? Because once she had loved him. She had loved him so much that she'd walked around with the biggest, stupidest smile on her face. She had felt dizzy with it, as if she'd been struck down by a mystery malady for which there was no known cure.

But it was hard to see things in a balanced way once you started looking at them from a distance. She'd got out of the habit of remembering the good times and that had been intentional. You could never move on if you allowed yourself to wallow in something which you were never going to have again.

'No, I didn't think about that,' she said. 'Even though I *did* find life hard without you. For quite a long time, actually. You're a big enough personality for the world to feel quite empty without you—and it did. But our marriage wasn't working, Xenon. You know it wasn't.'

He stared at her and his next words seemed to come

from some dark and unknown place deep inside him. 'Because of the baby.' There. He'd said it. He'd confronted something which had been too unbearable to confront at the time. Two long years had passed since it had happened and he had thought that time would have blunted the impact—but he was unprepared for the wave of pain which hit him with the force of a tsunami.

Lexi saw him flinch and she felt distress clawing away inside her as the hairbrush slipped from her suddenly nerveless fingers and clattered onto the dressing table. That old and familiar feeling of powerlessness swept over her and became all tangled up with her grief. She still felt guilty for the pain she had caused him by her inability to carry a child to term.

Thanks to her chronic insecurity and Xenon's demanding work schedule, communication between them had broken down. The first miscarriage had left an emptiness deep inside her and the second seemed to have brought everything to a head. She would never forget the bleakness etched on his face when he'd finally arrived at the hospital, once it was all over. The way he'd found it difficult to look her in the eye as he'd sat stiff and unmoving beside her bed.

But why hurt him more than he was already hurting by reminding him of that bitter time? It wouldn't change anything, would it?

Interlocking her fingers, she stared down at them and thought about all the games of cat's cradle she would never play with her child. 'I don't want to talk about it.'

'Why not?' He realised that his voice was shaking. 'Lex, look at me. Please.'

She lifted her head and it was almost unbearable to have to meet that bleak gaze of his. Why was he doing this now? Now when it was much too late. It was like picking at a scar and making the cut so deep that it would never heal. And how could she possibly heal if she started to fool herself that he wanted to *understand*? Because she knew better than anyone that Xenon didn't do understanding.

'Because it's too late,' she said, her fingers gripping at the shiny surface of the dressing table, as if she needed that small piece of leverage to prevent herself from sliding to the floor.

Stubbornly he shook his head as he stared at her, with a sense of determination he rarely felt outside the boardroom. After two years of having this fester away inside him like something dark and unmentionable, didn't it come as something of a relief to finally expunge it? 'Don't you think it's time we said all this? Stuff we couldn't bear to say at the time? Because you couldn't bear me to touch you after the second miscarriage, could you, Lex? You couldn't bear to let me near you.'

She got up from the dressing table and walked over to the window, wanting to put distance between them. Wanting to stop the pain which was twisting remorselessly inside her. She stared out as the first shadows of the evening began to deepen the summer night and they seemed to echo the darkness in her heart. 'Because I saw that look in your eyes!'

'What look?'

'What look? *What look?* You know damned well what look! The look that said I'd failed you—only this time I'd done it in spectacular style. I mean, I was already aware of the shortfall in my attempts to be the perfect wife, but this was one thing I really couldn't afford to get wrong, wasn't it?' She sucked in a ragged breath. 'And I did. You'd married me essentially to be your brood mare and you realised too late that you'd chosen a weak and flighty filly who was never going to meet your requirements.'

'Will you stop putting words in my mouth?'

She shook her head, resting her forehead against the coolness of the glass as her breath made it grow misty. 'Don't tell me that you haven't thought all these things, Xenon, because I won't believe you. Maybe in a way I don't blame you. I can even understand why you would think that.'

'Can you?' he questioned. 'You've added mind-reading to your sizeable list of accomplishments, have you?'

'Think about it,' she said, ignoring his sarcasm. 'You've devoted your entire adult life to growing the Kanellis corporation. And you need a son and heir to take over from you, as once you took over from your father and he from his father before him. You've always put having a family of your own at the top of your list of requirements.' She took a deep breath. 'We both know that.'

Her words were met with silence. She hadn't really

expected a denial, but the lack of one hurt her more than she had expected. For the first time in a long time, she wanted to cry. But she never cried in front of anyone, because tears got you nowhere and they made you look weak. They took you back to that scary place—the one which made you look into the future, and think about everything you were missing.

Outside the window the shadows in the park were lengthening. She saw a street-light flicker on, and then another. A young couple, arm in arm and laughing, walked past. It was as if the world were conspiring to remind her of everything she no longer had. It could be a cruel old world sometimes.

But she was doing this for Jason—that was the thought she needed to hang onto. She was giving her little brother a last chance to get his mixed-up life back on track. And if she and Xenon could manage to close the door on some of their *issues*, then wouldn't that be an added bonus? They might never become one of those divorced couples who were amicable enough to have dinner together—but mightn't they aim for some kind of civilised parting which didn't resemble a dark night of the soul?

Just so long as she realised that it wasn't going anywhere.

'I think you need dinner,' he said, his voice breaking into her thoughts.

She turned around to find him watching her closely. Too closely. 'I don't know that I'm very hungry.'

'Oh, no.' His voice was grim. 'I'm not having you

fainting on me when we fly to Rhodes tomorrow. You are going to eat, Lex—even if I have to find a spoon and feed you myself.'

She wanted to fight him but she knew he was right. Hunger made your thinking go haywire and that was the last thing she needed. She sighed. 'Okay, I'll eat. But I don't want to go and sit in some fancy restaurant. I can't face the thought of dressing up and having to sit with other people watching us. Or rather, watching you.' She gave a wry smile. 'I don't tend to attract unwanted attention these days.'

He glanced at her hair with curious eyes. 'Is that why you lost the red?'

'Partly. And I could no longer face going to the hairdressers' every six weeks to have my roots touched up.'

'That often?'

She smiled. 'Didn't you realise? That kind of glossy hair doesn't just happen by magic, no matter what the ads might promise.'

'And the glasses? Do you wear them because they make you look so different and reduce your chances of being recognised?'

'Actually, no. I wear them because they're good for all the detailed work I do with my jewellery design.' She found herself wondering whether he liked them or not, but Xenon's opinion of her trendy spectacles didn't count. *She* liked them and that was what mattered. She didn't add that she felt safer behind them. That their slightly geeky look fitted her new image of herself. 'And I was always losing my contact lenses.'

'Tell me about it,' he said. 'I seemed to spend half my time on my hands and knees looking for the damned things.' He gave a lazy smile. 'But I rather enjoyed being on the floor with you for what you might call legitimate purposes.'

Their eyes met.

'Xenon, don't.'

'Don't what?'

'Don't keep dredging up memories.' *Especially not happy ones.* 'There's no point.'

'Okay.' He lifted his hands in mock-surrender. 'The past is off-limits. Just come downstairs when you're ready and I'll fix dinner.'

'You?' Lexi blinked. 'Did I hear that correctly? Xenon Kanellis fixing dinner? Why, you wouldn't know where to start unless it involved speed-dialling the nearest Michelin-starred restaurant.'

'Want to bet?'

'I think I'll leave the betting to my brother.' She pulled a face. 'Or hopefully not. So what's on the menu? A take-out from the local deli?'

'Wait and see,' he responded coolly and walked out.

Lexi didn't move for a moment or two after the door had closed behind him. She wanted to go back over everything he'd said, and to replay it in her mind like a teenager with her first crush.

He'd thought she might want to give their marriage another go?

But—as she'd said—there was absolutely no point

dredging up memories and so she went into the bathroom, determined to wash all thoughts of him away.

Afterwards she put on a pair of jeans and gave her reflection a satisfied nod. Xenon wasn't a big fan of jeans because he thought it was a crime for a woman to cover up her legs. But if her legs were covered then he wouldn't look at them in the way she was discovering she still liked. And just to really slam the message home, she pulled on a baggy black T-shirt, with a giant pink sequinned lollipop on the front.

He had laid the table in the garden and lit lots of little tea-lights and she found that as astonishing as anything else which had happened. Xenon managing to put a match to tea-lights? Whatever next? Xenon discovering that food came from shops, and that you actually had to go and buy it?

But she was somewhat relieved to discover that the familiar macho Xenon was never too far from the surface because when she walked into the garden, he looked up and scowled.

'What's that hideous thing you're wearing?'

She affected innocence as she ran a reflective forefinger over the garish pink sequins. 'This? It's one of a batch from our last tour, which never got sold. Extra-extra-large. If you're interested I can always have one couriered to you. I've got masses of them back at the cottage.'

He gave a flicker of a smile as he poured a glass of wine and handed it to her. 'Tempting, but I'll pass. Now, eat.'

She sat down and did as he suggested and was soon tucking into pasta with a simple sauce, studded with anchovies and olives. Afterwards there were iced grapes and squares of dark chocolate, accompanied by the thick, sweet coffee he loved so much. In the flickering light, she ate with an appetite which seemed sharpened, and as the stars began to prick the velvet sky she felt better.

By tacit agreement, they kept to neutral topics, with Xenon recounting some of the exploits of his twin cousins in New York, who Lexi had always liked. He told her that there had been talk of doing a sequel to *My Crazy Greek Father* but that he had ruled it out, because he couldn't face going back to Hollywood for any sustained length of time. Lexi found herself wishing that the dinner could continue, like one of those meals you found in fairy tales, where the table was lavishly replenished each day. Because around that table it was easy to forget about the world which existed outside that garden.

But the world did exist and it came with complications. Big complications, in their case. She pushed away her empty coffee cup and looked at him.

'What have you told your mother?'

He shrugged. 'That you're coming to the christening with me and are eager to see my grandmother again. Other than that, I haven't elaborated.'

She folded her napkin and put it on the table. 'And what did she say?'

For a moment Xenon was silent as he poured himself another cup of coffee. Unsurprisingly, his mother's response to his news had been muted. She had never wanted him to marry this particular Englishwoman when there had been so many suitable Greek girls eager to take on that privileged role. He suspected she still lived in hope that it might one day still happen, for she did not share his grandmother's sentimental views on divorce. But he had told her that Lexi's visit was non-negotiable and had demanded that she show his estranged wife courtesy and consideration, a demand which had left his mother looking at him thoughtfully before she had agreed.

'She accepted it,' he said.

'Just like that?'

He raised his eyebrows. 'My mother wouldn't dream of objecting to the way I live my life. Not any more.'

'Or maybe she just wouldn't dream of saying it out loud.'

'Most people have thoughts they wouldn't want to say out loud, Lex. I'm having a few of my own at the moment.'

She stood up. 'I think that's my cue for bed.'

'Wise decision.' His eyes gleamed. 'If a rather disappointing one as far as I'm concerned.'

Lexi looked at his ruggedly handsome face and thought how easy it would be if they'd only just met. If she could just give in to the demands of her body. Just walk right over there and let him take her in his arms and to hell with the consequences.

But she couldn't. There was a reason why she still sometimes woke in the middle of the night with her heart pounding with fear and a sinking feeling of realisation twisting at her gut.

It was the same reason why she could never give their marriage another go.

CHAPTER FIVE

THE FAINT DRONE of the aircraft engine was the only sound he could hear and several times Xenon found himself lifting his head from his pile of paperwork, to see if Lexi had fallen asleep. She hadn't. She was sitting staring at an open magazine on her lap, though he noticed she hadn't turned a single page.

She still looked pale, he thought. Against her flowery dress her skin seemed almost transparent, giving her a delicate appearance which made her seem almost breakable. But she wasn't breakable, he reminded himself. Behind her delicate appearance, she was tough. The toughest woman he had ever known.

He looked down at the document but the words were just a blur of black and white. He leaned his head back against the seat. Last night they'd talked more frankly about the baby than they'd ever done before—but he had been left with no answers. Maybe there were no answers. Maybe he just had to learn to accept that it was what it was. A marriage against which the odds had been stacked from the beginning, followed by circumstances which had conspired to prove it was never going to work.

Yet that wasn't helping him deal with the current situation, was it? It didn't stop him wanting her so badly that it was all he could do not to reach out and touch her. She'd made it clear that sex wasn't on her agenda but he wondered how long her resolve would last once they were back to sharing a bedroom.

The engine noise changed and he glanced out of the cabin window. 'Look, we're coming in to land,' he said.

Lexi followed the direction of his gaze and saw the island of Rhodes dazzling like a bright jewel in the dark blue waters of the Aegean. She thought how long it had been since she'd been abroad and done anything as decadent as just lie in the sun. 'When were you last here?'

'I came over a couple of months ago for a few days. Work has been...demanding.'

'So what else is new?' she demanded wryly. 'You haven't stopped since we boarded the plane.'

His blue eyes gleamed. 'There's a reason for that. I've been trying to clear my diary so that I won't need to work while we're here.'

Lexi felt her lips part in surprise. 'Good heavens,' she said faintly. 'Next thing you'll be telling me that you're planning to switch off your phone at night.'

'If that's a veiled offer to share my bed, then consider it done.'

'It wasn't.'

He smiled. 'Didn't think so.'

He picked up the documents and put them in his

briefcase, vowing not to go near them for the duration of their stay. But it was hard to break the habit of a life-time—a way of living and working which had become second nature to him.

He'd been barely eighteen when his father had dropped dead and Xenon's discovery that the business was in a parlous state hadn't helped the family come to terms with their shock and grief. Suddenly, the world as he had known it was one he no longer recognised.

But he had turned everything around. He had thrown himself in at the deep end and worked every hour to learn about the business, from the bottom up. He had sweated blood to earn the respect of the disillusioned Kanellis workforce. And while most people would have been content simply to get the giant organisation back on its feet, Xenon was not most people. He didn't want to be known as a man who had saved something, he wanted to be known as a man who had made something. That was why he had bought the newspaper.

The film had been something different. The film had touched something deep inside him. It had con-nected with his essential *Greekness*. He had backed it because he had loved it; the money and awards he had earned as a result had not been what had driven him. And Lexi had understood. She had loved that film, too.

'I'm trying to learn how to delegate,' he said and saw her turn her head to look at him, that lip-parted look of surprise still on her face. 'Loukas and Dimitri are keen to share some of the responsibility but it's hard to let go when I've lived this way for so long.'

'What are you so scared of.'

The smile which greeted this remark was sardonic. 'You think that I am scared? That Xenon Kanellis is scared of anything?'

'Well, if you're not—then why not just go ahead and do it? Free up more time for yourself. Enjoy some of the fruits of your labours.' Her voice softened. 'Didn't you once tell me that you weren't going to work yourself into an early grave, like your father?'

He stared into her eyes, which looked as silvery-cool as mercury. What would she say if he told her that these days the hours he worked filled an emptiness which nothing else seemed to touch? That sometimes he held onto work with the determination of a man clutching at a lifeline?

But introspection had never been his thing. He had always preferred the practical to the theoretical. He caught hold of her hand and turned it over. 'Where's your wedding ring?'

'At home, somewhere.'

'Or maybe you threw it away in a bid to forget me— isn't that what bitter ex-wives do?'

'Actually, it's in a box on top of my dressing table, along with all the other jewellery I no longer wear. And I'm not bitter, Xenon.'

'You should have brought it with you.' He traced an imaginary ring with the tip of his finger. 'What if my grandmother notices you aren't wearing it?'

'She'll have to draw her own conclusions.'

'I disagree. We'll have to see about finding you another one.'

His words were distracting and so was his touch and Lexi was glad to pull her hand away and scrabble around in her bag for her passport and wallet.

Fast-tracked through customs, Xenon was treated like a homecoming king and greeted fondly by airport workers he'd known since he was a boy. Lexi had forgotten how he could lay on the charm and get people eating out of his hand—especially here in his homeland. He possessed an ability to blend in no matter what the company and could happily drink with socialites and lorry-drivers alike. Hadn't he once managed to avert a dockers' strike by the simple expedient of walking into the shipyard and talking to the union chief over a cup of coffee?

Outside the terminal a car was waiting and Xenon said something in Greek to the driver as they pulled away. They'd been driving for about ten minutes when Lexi realised they were going the wrong way.

'This isn't the way to your home.'

'I know it isn't. We're going into Rhodes Town first.'

She'd begun to feel nervous at the thought of seeing his family again and the thought of a delay was only adding to her anxiety levels. 'What for?'

'Have patience, Lex. Just sit back and enjoy the scenery, and let me take care of it.'

Lexi glowered. There he was, doing that dominant macho thing again—and she was just letting him get away with it. And yet it was frighteningly easy to sink back into the soft leather seat and drink in the beautiful views which were flashing past the window. Before long they had reached Rhodes Town and, since Xenon's driver was experienced enough to skilfully negotiate the busy streets, the car was soon sliding to a halt outside a small jeweller's shop.

Lexi saw the glint of precious metals and diamonds glittering in the window and she frowned. 'What's going on?'

'Simple. You're missing a wedding ring, so we're buying you a new one.'

'No,' she said desperately. 'We're not.'

But the driver was already opening her door and, other than creating a very public scene, what choice did she have other than to step out onto the hot pavement? How could she put into words without sounding stupidly vulnerable that she didn't want a *pretend* ring. She didn't want anything that was going to make an even bigger mockery of her failed marriage.

But Xenon was really in control mode by then, busy speaking in Greek to the shop's owner who swiftly produced a velvet tray of rings—some plain, some embellished and all of them extremely costly, judging by the price-tags.

Did the man notice her marked lack of enthusiasm and wonder why she wasn't happy or triumphant to have such an eligible man fussing over her? Did he notice her flinch as Xenon masterminded the whole operation, his gaze flicking over the tray with the eye of the connoisseur as he made suggestions about what kind of ring she'd prefer. But she couldn't really walk out of there empty-handed and so in the end she chose the simplest of them all—a discreet band in eighteen-carat gold.

'Try not to lose *this* one, darling,' murmured Xenon in English. Picking up the ring, he slid it slowly onto her finger, his blue eyes narrowing behind the lush curtain of his lashes as if he had felt the automatic tensing of her hand.

As Xenon's payment card was being processed, the shop owner leaned forward to admire the clunky silver bangle which was dangling from Lexi's wrist.

'This is beautiful,' he said.

'My wife makes jewellery,' put in Xenon helpfully.

Lexi shot him a furious look, thinking that he was getting carried away. He didn't *need* to play the proud husband in front of someone they were never going to see again.

The shopkeeper nodded. 'You sell anything here on Rhodes?'

'No. Only in England,' she said, with a smile.

'You want to bring me some pieces to look at? I'm always on the lookout for original work. Tourists like to spend money when they are on holiday.'

She opened her mouth to explain that her visit here was temporary, but once again Xenon butted in.

'We have rather a busy schedule at the moment, don't we, darling?'

Lexi wanted to drum her fists against his chest and tell him that she was not his darling. She wanted to tear the fake wedding ring from her finger and hurl it down on the counter, but she respected Xenon's position within the local community, even if he didn't respect her feelings. She began to wonder how on earth she was going to maintain this crazy façade for more than a minute when he seemed determined to get under her skin at every opportunity.

The walls of the shop felt as if they were closing in on her and, deliberately, she looked at her watch. 'We really ought to be going,' she said.

They stepped outside into the sunlight and Lexi was just about to give him a piece of her mind when a flare of white, incandescent light almost blinded her. A man dressed in denim leapt out from the side of the building and began firing off a rapid series of photos, pushing a giant camera in her face.

For a moment they were both too startled to move before Xenon swore at him.

'What the hell?' he snarled, making a lunge for the camera.

But although he was fast, the photographer had the element of surprise on his side. He sprinted off and jumped onto the back of a waiting motorbike, which began to weave its way up the street before roaring off into the distance, lost to sight.

'I'm going after him!' Xenon snarled, but Lexi clamped a restraining hand on his bunched arm.

'How? Not by foot, you won't—and you'll never catch him in this enormous car!' But she was shaking. Shaking like a leaf. She hadn't been ambushed like that in a long time and she had forgotten how exposed it could make you feel. She could see several tourists stopping now and, inevitably, some of them were getting their phones out. 'Now look what's happening,' she moaned.

'Get in the car,' said Xenon, pushing her into the back seat before sliding in beside her.

Once they'd pulled away he took out his mobile phone, punched out a number and began speaking in a flurry of Greek for several furious minutes. The call finished, he turned to her. 'Perhaps I should have anticipated that might happen. I'm sorry.'

'Well, it's a bit late to be sorry,' she said crossly, trying not to melt beneath the genuine contrition in his blue eyes. 'That was a gift of a photo. Why, I could even write the headlines for them: *Greek Billionaire And Ex-Wife Ring The Changes.*'

'That's very good, Lex. Did you ever think about a career in copywriting?'

'Don't you dare try and make a joke about it. Didn't you stop to think that someone might have seen us going into a *jewellery shop* and rung the press?'

'Oddly enough, the press aren't my first priority. I don't spend my damned life tiptoeing around them.'

'Well, maybe you should. Now they'll think there's a story when there isn't. A divorcing couple buying a brand-new wedding ring! Why don't we find somewhere where I can buy a white dress and a bunch of flowers and we can maybe pose for some more photos?'

'Stop worrying.' His voice was soothing. 'I've sorted it.'

'How?'

'Just leave it to me.'

To Lexi's surprise, the journey passed quickly and suddenly the magnificent Kanellis estate was coming into view—a glorious citadel overlooking the medieval town of Lindos. But despite the beauty which surrounded her, Lexi felt her body tense as the car drove through the electronic gates before coming to a halt in the main courtyard.

Because she still had to face Marina, didn't she? And hadn't that always been a stumbling block?

Xenon's mother hadn't been her biggest fan. She clearly disapproved of a flashy English pop-star with a troubled background. It didn't matter what Lexi did—or what she tried to do—she was never able to do it right. Toning down her image and trying to blend into an aristocratic Greek background was never going to work. She'd never broken through that initial barrier of hostility and it seemed that her mother-in-law could never get past the fact that she thought her beloved son had married beneath him.

But that was no longer relevant, Lexi told herself. *I'm doing this for Jason. And I am no longer that woman who is so easily intimidated.*

'Here we are,' said Xenon. He caught her gaze and held it. 'Ready?'

She drew in a breath. 'Ready as I'll ever be.'

The driver opened the door for her and she stepped out into the sunny central courtyard where she was immediately enveloped in warm, fragrant air.

Looking down she could see the crystal waters of St Nicolas Bay and the hills which framed it like a picture. She could smell pine and lemons and hear the magnified hum of the cicadas. It was so typically and beautifully Greek that for a moment Lexi just stood there, drinking in the moment.

The land had been owned by the family for centuries and the tiered estate was vast and sprawling. All three of its bougainvillea-covered properties were entirely separate—each with their own private gardens. Pots of tumbling flowers provided splashes of colour—and the infinity pool seemed to connect with the sea and sky in layers of different, dazzling blues. Lexi had often wondered what it must have been like to have grown up in a place as beautiful as this. A place which was as different from the scruffy social housing where she'd spent her formative years as night was to day.

Suddenly she saw a familiar figure emerging from the main house, the sun illuminating the new threads of grey which were streaking her dark hair.

Her workaday dress was covered with an apron and Lexi's heart clenched in her chest as the woman grew closer. 'Phyllida!' she croaked—and then all the breath was knocked out of her lungs as she was caught in a fierce embrace by Xenon's London housekeeper.

For a few moments the women hugged but didn't speak and Lexi was glad because the lump in her throat would have made speech impossible. Because it had been Phyllida who had been with her in London the night Lexi had started to bleed. Phyllida who had rung for the doctor and accompanied Lexi to hospital when the pain had got so bad and nobody could get hold of Xenon.

Lexi felt the memories come flooding back. There had been no one else she had trusted enough to ask at the time. Her first miscarriage had been so early—at eight weeks it had been more like a very heavy though heartbreaking period. But the second time had been different.

All her hopes and dreams had been focused on the life growing inside her and when that first low cramping pain had caught her by surprise, she had been so *scared*. She hadn't been able to believe it was happening all over again—especially because she'd passed the 'danger' period of twelve weeks. But it had been happening and there wasn't a thing she could do to stop it. It had been the Greek housekeeper who had kept a silent vigil throughout the day and into the next day, until at long last Xenon had arrived back from his trip to the Far East. He had walked into her private room at the hospital and Lexi had seen the empty look in his eyes when she told him that the baby had died. And she had known that nothing was ever going to be the same again.

She drew back from the housekeeper's embrace and took a moment to compose herself. 'Oh, Phyllida,' she said. 'I can't tell you how good it is to see you again.'

'Kyrios Alexi.' Clearly emotional herself, Phyllida touched Lexi's hair. 'You have changed.'

'No longer the crazy redhead? I know. While you look exactly the same. You look fantastic.'

'No. I am too fat.' Phyllida laughed as she patted her ample stomach. 'Not like you.'

Xenon glanced across at the main house. 'Is my mother around?' he asked.

'She went to visit your sister. She said that you should settle in and she will see you at dinner.'

Xenon's voice dropped. 'And my grandmother?'

Phyllida shook her head, her face growing grave. 'She is weak, but she is comfortable,' she said. 'The nurse is with her now and she is looking forward to seeing her grandson again. Now. Shall I make fresh lemonade for you and Kyrios Alexi after your long journey?'

'Efharisto,' said Xenon, his hand moving to brush the base of Lexi's spine. 'Come on, Lex. Let's go and unpack.'

It was the briefest of touches but it started a whisper of reaction flaring over her skin and Lexi could feel her heart pounding as she followed him towards the furthest of the three villas, with its prime position overlooking the bay.

Their cases had been deposited inside the house and left on the ghostly surface of the marble floor—standing side by side as if in silent mockery. The white walls and dark wooden furniture were just as she remembered and Phyllida must have put that vase of white roses on one of the low tables.

The door of the villa closed behind them and Lexi was left with a feeling of panic. She thought of the bedroom next door and unwanted memories came crowding back. The smell of sex and the rumpled sheets. The closeness of Xenon's hard body.

She licked her tongue over impossibly dry lips before she spoke.

'Xenon, this is crazy. There's no way we can stay here.'

'Why not?'

'You know very well why not. You're not a stupid man, although at times you can be a very stubborn one.' She steeled herself against the soft light of battle on his face. *Don't make me spell it out,* her eyes pleaded silently. But his blue gaze remained obdurate and she glared at him. 'There's only one bed,' she said.

'And? Isn't the whole point that we're here as a married couple—and married couples share beds? What did you think would happen, Lex? That I would stay in the main house, knowing that you were closeted in here all on your own?'

'You could do what any other man would do under the circumstances—and offer to sleep on the sofa!'

He shot a disparaging look at the piece of furniture she was indicating. 'On that? Come on—that was never designed to be slept on. A Greek husband sleeps in the marital bed.' His blue eyes gleamed with a mixture of mockery and promise. 'With his wife.'

Lexi *hated* the way her body responded to the unashamedly sexual look which accompanied his macho boast. It was easy to tell herself she shouldn't want him but much harder to ignore the way he was making her feel. When his gaze raked over her like that, she could feel the answering clamour of her body. The ache of her breasts and the insistent heat coiling low inside her. Because she still desired him as intensely as she had ever done—and she didn't have a clue how to deal with it.

'Why did you bring me here, Xenon?' she demanded. 'I mean, *really*? You say it was to bring comfort to your grandmother—'

'That desire was genuine,' he interrupted coolly.

'And what else? Did you picture this scene when you made your suggestion? The inevitable showdown which would result when I found out that I'd be expected to share a bed with you?'

For a moment he didn't answer and when he did, his words were accompanied by an odd kind of smile. 'Yes, I pictured it,' he answered slowly. 'Though not at first.'

She stared at him, her heart beating very fast. 'Tell me.'

He lifted his shoulders in a careless kind of shrug and once again she could see the bunching of muscle beneath his shirt. 'I admit that when I came to your house that day I was little more than curious. I wanted to see the woman I had married and to see what life had done to her. I'd even promised myself that I would give you your divorce papers, if I were so inclined. And then you opened the door and...'

His voice tailed off in a way which made Lexi look at him suspiciously. Because Xenon didn't do hesitation. And neither did he screw his eyes up as if he had been presented with a problem he couldn't quite work out. Because wasn't he the man with the answers to everything?

'And what?' she prompted.

'I realised I still wanted you,' he said simply. 'I wanted you in a way I've never wanted any other woman, not before and not since. I wanted you in my arms. I still do. I look at you, Lex, and my body aches for you. I want you so badly that I can hardly think straight. Even now.'

She felt the dull crash of disappointment—for these were not new words. They were words he'd spoken many times when he'd been wooing her—when she'd bewitched and infuriated him by refusing to fall straight into his arms. They were expressions of high emotion he used when he was trying to get something which was just out of reach. He'd never said them when they would have meant something. He'd hadn't spoken of wanting her when she'd been lying in that hospital bed with her womb raw and empty and the feeling that she had failed him as a wife.

'We can't,' she said in a hollow voice.

'Why not?' he demanded, his eyes blazing like blue jewels in the dimness of the shuttered room. 'Because you haven't got the guts to face the fact that you want me, too? Why can't you just come out and admit it? If not to me—then at least to yourself. That what we have isn't over. And that it isn't going to go away.'

She felt the quickening stab of fear and the even fiercer stab of desire. She felt the blurring of past and present. She thought about the secrets she had locked away.

'You just like a challenge,' she declared. 'You're a man who has everything. Who can get anything. You just want the one thing that's eluding you.'

'This has got nothing to do with challenge,' he said, his eyes narrowing as he met the spark of defiance in hers. He was aware of something primitive flooding through him. A tide of pure possession which he could not stop. 'And everything to do with the realisation that you are my woman and you always have been. And nothing will ever change that.'

The raw declaration thrilled her almost more than it appalled her. She wouldn't have been human if it hadn't. But Lexi knew that she couldn't be swayed by words which were driven by nothing more than lust and a sense of ownership.

'I can't do it,' she said. 'We can share a bed and maintain this charade if that's what it takes to get my brother off the hook, but that's all.' With an effort she tried to ignore the prickling of her breasts. The way that they had become heavy and sensitive—as if they wanted nothing more than for him to bend his lips to kiss them, shaping his lips around them and tormenting her with the feathery little lick of his tongue.

She shivered, trying to blot the erotic image from her mind and to focus on something other than the sudden hot, melting ache between her legs. 'It's over, Xenon,' she croaked. 'There's no way back. And there's no way I'm ever getting intimate with you again.'

CHAPTER SIX

'SO, ALEXI. MY son tells me that you are something of a silversmith these days.'

Lexi put her wine glass down and produced another friendly smile, even though her face was beginning to ache. She felt like someone who had undergone a police interrogation, since Xenon's mother had been firing questions at her for most of the overlong meal. And her arrogant son hadn't done a thing to help her out.

Dressed impeccably in navy, with pearls gleaming at her throat, Marina Kanellis was an elegant woman whose once-beautiful face bore a vaguely startled look, as if life had disappointed her. Lexi knew she'd been made a widow when Xenon was barely eighteen and not for the first time she wondered why the bilingual socialite had never considered marrying again. Unless she was one of those women who loved only one man...

This line of thought was a little too uncomfortable to pursue. Instead Lexi concentrated on watching the candlelight flickering over the heavy crystal and silver, telling herself that the meal would soon be over and then she would be able to make her escape. She had tried to answer her mother-in-law's queries as cheerfully as possible—even though she had been chewed up with nerves when she'd first sat down.

Yet she couldn't deny that tonight Marina had seemed almost *kind* and much less terrifying than before. Maybe that was because these days she felt more mature and much less intimidated. And, of course, less worried that she was going to make some terrible social gaffe and make Xenon ashamed of her. She no longer had anything to lose, did she?

So she turned to Marina Kanellis and smiled.

'"Silversmith" sounds a bit grand for what I do,' she said.

'But you are making jewellery?'

Lexi nodded, her fingertips brushing against the two elongated silver triangles dangling from her ears as if she were showcasing her handiwork. 'Yes, I am.'

'And you enjoy it?' asked Marina.

'I love it,' Lexi answered. 'I've got my own little workshop in the village and I enjoy being my own boss. It gives me the kind of freedom I've never had before.'

'I can imagine.' Marina Kanellis sipped from her glass of water. 'I never worked, of course. Not before my marriage nor after it. It was not considered appropriate for a woman to work, particularly if she was a Kanellis woman, with all the responsibilities which went with that role.'

Lexi looked into Xenon's piercing blue eyes. *Help me out here,* she beseeched him silently and to her astonishment she saw an answering glint of comprehension.

'Modern women like to work, *Mitera*,' he said, with the tone of somebody who had made the recent discovery that the world was round. 'Some obviously need to work for economic reasons—but others do it because it gives them a purpose in life. It fulfils them in a way that nothing else can—something which men have known for centuries. And who are we to knock that?'

Lexi wondered if her own expression reflected the dazed bemusement of her mother-in-law's. She looked across the table at her husband in disbelief. Xenon coming out with an opinion about women which didn't sound as if it had been formed two centuries ago? This from the man who had been adamant that she should be a stay-at-home wife?

At the time, he had explained that they had far too much money for his conscience to allow her to work. Which in theory Lexi had tried to understand. She had told herself that she had married a Greek and that she had to accept there would be cultural differences.

But what did a woman do all day when she wasn't working and there were servants to run her life for her? Especially if she was a woman who didn't like to 'do' lunch, or spend hours shopping?

She waited to become a mother, that was what she did. And while she waited—in vain, in her case—she discovered that Xenon was governed less by his conscience than by his need to control her and his possessive desire to know where she was at any hour of the day.

So had he changed his views, or was he simply expressing something different because it was expedient for him to do so?

She met his eyes and saw the unexpected flash of humour glittering in their blue depths as if he knew perfectly well the thoughts which were running through her head. That lazy smile of comprehension flustered her and she turned to her mother-in-law, deliberately changing the subject. 'I'm sorry to hear that your mother is so ill,' she said quietly.

Marina Kanellis nodded and then sighed. 'I know. She is old, of course, and she has lived a good life,' she said. 'But that makes it no less painful for those of us who love her. We must just make sure that she is kept comfortable, and happy. You will go and see her tomorrow?'

'Yes, I will. I'd like that very much,' said Lexi.

'You know, she always enjoyed your songs,' said Marina unexpectedly. 'Especially the one about the man who got away.'

'"Come Right Back",' said Lexi instantly, but this time she didn't dare look across the table at Xenon. Didn't they say that there was nothing as potent as cheap music—and hadn't the words of that particular song seemed unbearably poignant for a long time after they'd split?

But her mood by the end of dinner was much more mellow than the one with which she'd begun it and the excellent food and rich Kanellis wine left her feeling warm and replete.

After the meal they sat outside and drank coffee on

the terrace, overlooking the bay. The sky was as dark as a railway tunnel but it was punctured by the diamond dazzle of a thousand stars. She looked down at the lights of Lindos and the glitter of the Aegean and wished she could freeze that moment and never have it melt.

But after she'd said goodnight to Marina and walked with Xenon back to their villa, Lexi began to get butterfly feelings of nerves fluttering around inside her.

She avoided any kind of confrontation until after she'd brushed her teeth and tackled the time-consuming task of brushing her long hair. By the time she'd emerged from the bathroom, it was to find Xenon standing by the bedroom window, staring out at the glittering sea.

He turned round when she entered even though her bare feet must have made hardly any sound on the marble floor. He gave the glimmer of a smile when he saw she was covered from neck to ankle in a pair of pale silk pyjamas, but he made no comment about her buttoned-up nightwear.

'You were sweet with my mother tonight,' he said.

Lexi blinked. It wasn't what she had been expecting to hear. What *had* she been expecting? 'She's much softer than she used to be.'

'Yes, she is. So many things have happened and she's a grandmother now. I think the fact that her own mother is dying has made her look at the world differently.' He shrugged. 'The cycle of life keeps turning. It's made her aware of how precious time is.'

His undeniably emotional words hung on the air and

Lexi felt the painful punch of her heart. 'No. None of us should ever forget that,' she said.

Xenon let his gaze drift over her. She had taken off her glasses and her face was scrubbed clean. He thought how unbelievably young she looked. And how innocent. Sometimes it was hard to believe the reality of her rough upbringing when right now she looked as if she'd spent her life growing up in a convent, nurtured on nothing stronger than milk and orange juice. Her fair hair tumbled down over her pyjamas and he wondered what she would say if he told her that the look she'd been aiming for had completely missed the mark. Because it didn't matter how prim she tried to make herself—she still exuded a sensuality which oozed from her like honey from a slice of Baklava.

'Ready for bed?' he questioned sardonically.

'What do you think?'

'I don't think you want to know what I think. So why don't you run along and make yourself comfortable and I'll give you long enough so that you can pretend to be asleep when I join you?'

Lexi's face felt hot as she skulked off into the bedroom and climbed in between the Egyptian cotton sheets and for a moment she felt *foolish*. Had that been deliberate on his part? Was Xenon trying to make her doubt herself? Trying to make her believe that any woman would be insane not to take advantage of the opportunity which was now presenting itself?

Was she? Would it really be the end of the world if she gave in and let him make love to her again?

She knew the answer immediately. Of course it would. It would take her back to that dark place, the one with the unimaginable future and constant heartache. *So forget it,* she told herself fiercely.

Instead, she lay there doing a crash-course in sheep-counting and listening to the distant swish of the shower. And maybe she was wearier than she'd thought, because her eyelids began to grow heavy. Or maybe Xenon was just keeping to his word and stalling for as long as possible.

All she knew was that by the time he came to bed, she was in that comfortable half-world between waking and sleeping and the dip in the mattress as he got in beside her didn't alarm her as much as it should have done.

But then he moved and she became aware of just how much space his body took up, even though the bed was vast. It had been a long time since she'd slept with him and her space suddenly seemed to have been invaded by a potent rush of testosterone. She could sense it pulsing in the air around her; she could feel her skin absorbing it, like a dark sensual heat.

She held her breath for what must have been a full minute while they lay there in the darkness, until his drawled voice broke the silence.

'So are we just going to lie here, pretending to be asleep?'

She let out her breath in a slow rush. 'I'm not going to ask what your alternative suggestion might be.'

'You might be surprised by the answer. Come here.' Snaking out his hand, he pulled her against him so that her bottom was pushed against his belly and his hand was resting lazily over the jut of her hip bone.

Half-heartedly, Lexi wriggled. 'Don't.'

'Don't make such a big deal out of it, Lex. Relax. I'm just holding you, that's all.'

She wanted to tell him to roll over to the far side of the bed and leave her alone, but something stopped her. Because wasn't it delicious to feel his warm breath fanning the back of her neck like that? And didn't his arm feel so *right* when it was lying around her waist? She wanted to wriggle closer, to settle herself comfortably in a spoonlike position against him as she'd done so many times before, but in the midst of this forbidden pleasure came confusion. Because this was a first. Xenon lying next to her and just *holding* her? What was that all about?

She closed her eyes. Her Greek husband had been very definite in his views about what took place in the marital bed and what took place was sex. Lots of it. Consistently amazing sex it had been, too. In fact, lying here with him just a hair's breadth away from her, it was very hard not to remember just how amazing it had been.

Until after the baby, of course. When Xenon had put himself out of 'temptation's way' by absenting himself from the marital bed and going to sleep in the room next door. He'd told her she needed time to recover, but in her sorrow and her grief Lexi had felt neglected, and lonely. The longer they had been apart, the easier it had been to stay that way. And then she'd had time to think that maybe it was all for the best.

She had never slept with him again.

The taste of memory was bitter in her mouth and again she tried to wriggle away from him, but Xenon was having none of it. 'Relax,' he repeated.

'Trying to lull me into a false state of security isn't going to work.'

'How very brutal of you, Lex—to suggest that I might have some kind of ulterior motive.'

'Haven't you?'

'Not right at this moment, no.' Fractionally, his thumb moved over her satin-covered waist. 'Tell me, did you enjoy dinner?'

'Which part? The delicious *bourekakia* and *tiro-pita*—or your astonishing about-face on the subject of married women working?'

The thumb stopped moving. She thought she heard him sigh.

'I should never have stopped you from following your career,' he said.

Lexi stared into the nothingness. Now that her eyes were growing accustomed to the darkness, she could make out faint shapes of furniture. 'Nobody can stop someone from doing something, not if they don't want to.'

'But I delivered an ultimatum,' he said. 'I told you in no uncertain terms that I wouldn't tolerate my wife working.'

'And maybe you weren't entirely wrong,' she said

slowly. 'Our marriage would never have survived me trying to pursue a solo career which was always doomed. I recognised that eventually. It was just the way that you told me which hurt so much.'

'How?'

His word seemed to fill the dark room and Lexi's breathing grew shallow. It was a question he would never normally have asked, though this particular situation hardly qualified as 'normal', did it? Not by anyone's definition of the word. And surely the concealing cloak of darkness meant that she could answer it honestly.

'You spoke to me like I was just…*something* instead of someone,' she said. 'Like I was a person who was simply there to complement your life. As if I didn't have any feelings of my own. As if my singing career could just be flushed away. It was all about you, Xenon—it was only ever about you.'

As the breath left his lungs in an even heavier sigh Xenon could feel the ripple of her hair. He scowled into the darkness as her body tensed and he felt the bitter pain of regret—the sense that he had been blind to what had been right beneath his nose. Was it too late to tell her that? To tell her that he hadn't known how to behave any differently?

'I had certain expectations of marriage,' he said. 'Which I expected you, as my wife, to meet.'

'Yes, I know all that. You wanted a genteel woman. A yes-woman, yet you couldn't have chosen someone more different if you'd tried. I was from a totally different background. I'd clawed my way up from the bottom.

I'd looked after myself—and my brothers—all my life. I didn't know how to be anything *but* independent and yet suddenly you expected me to relinquish all that.'

'I wanted to look after you,' he said.

'No. You wanted to keep me in a cage. A highly embellished cage, it's true—but a cage no less. At first I didn't even notice. I was so enthralled by you—so happy just to *be* with you that if you'd suggested we live in a cave at the bottom of the garden I suspect I would have agreed.'

He flinched as he heard the way she said it. As if she couldn't believe the person she'd been back then. The person who had adored him. *Had.* 'I'd never been in love before,' he said slowly. 'I'd never been married before. All I knew was that wives were treated with a certain degree of reverence.'

In the darkness, Lexi gave a wry smile. 'Suppressing someone's spontaneity and talent isn't being reverential, Xenon—it's being controlling. Maybe you should face up to reality and accept that you're just not the marrying kind—or maybe you should try marrying a more conventional type of woman. One who likes to be manipulated like that.'

He let his mouth sink into her hair and his words were muffled by its silken richness. 'I'm sorry, Lex,' he said. 'Can you believe me when I say that to you?'

Lexi swallowed. The long silence seemed amplified by the darkness and the fact that she sensed he was holding his breath while he waited for an answer. It would be so much easier if she *didn't* believe him. If she thought that he was simply saying something because it was convenient for him to do so. But she knew Xenon well enough to recognise his words as genuine—and these were very powerful words indeed. 'Yes,' she said. 'I believe you.'

'And can you forgive me?'

Lexi closed her eyes. That was a harder question. Because forgiveness was complicated. When you forgave someone you left a vacuum where all the anger had been, and then what did you replace it with?

But she couldn't carry on fighting him simply because she was scared of her own feelings, could she? 'Yes,' she whispered, but she pulled away from him— not wanting him to interpret her clemency as some kind of sexual green light.

Xenon felt her move away and his body stiffened with the hot stab of frustration. His hand was still at her waist but he sensed she had withdrawn from him in more than a physical sense. Where a few minutes ago she had been warm and—he thought—on the verge of compliance, all that had now gone.

It very nearly killed him but he forced himself to drop nothing more than a light kiss onto her silk-covered shoulder and then to turn over. He had never done this in his life—stopped himself from taking what he wanted to take. What deep down he still considered it his *right* to take.

Scowling into the darkness, he moved over to the other side of the bed.

But sleep was a long time coming.

CHAPTER SEVEN

THE SHOWER WAS icy and Xenon stood beneath the punishing jets as he tried to rid his heated body of a desire so fierce that he felt he might explode with it. Tipping his head back, he allowed the impact of the cold water to power onto his face, but nothing could take away the thought that he had just spent an entire night in bed with his wife.

And he hadn't laid a finger on her.

He had lain awake as he'd felt the slide of her pyjama-clad body occasionally brushing up against him and the temptation to imprison her beneath him had been overpowering. He'd had to resist the urge to bury his fingers into her thick hair and to open his mouth over hers, kissing her until he had melted away every single one of her reservations.

He uttered a growled curse in Greek.

Would he see any signs of change in her this morning? he wondered. Would the frank discussion they'd had last night under cover of darkness have softened Lex's stance towards him?

She must have used the second bathroom because

when he returned to the bedroom with only a white towel wrapped around his hips she was no longer lying in bed where he'd left her. Wise woman, he thought grimly. It was probably safer to stay away from him when he was feeling like this.

He dressed and walked out onto the terrace to find her sitting at the table, wearing a simple cotton dress with her ponytailed hair hanging down her back. In front of her was a pot of coffee, a dish of Greek yoghurt and a platter of fruit. She looked up as he approached and, although her sunglasses concealed the expression in her eyes, he saw the way that her teeth chewed nervously at her bottom lip.

'What a touchingly domestic scene,' he drawled.

'I went over to the main house and got all this stuff from Phyllida,' she explained a little defensively, in response to the arrogant rise of his eyebrows. 'I thought it might be nice to have breakfast here, since the gardens are so pretty.'

He sat down and took the cup which she slid towards him. 'I imagined my mother planned for us to eat in the main house—but if you're planning to play housewife, that's fine by me.'

'I'm planning a little space,' she said firmly, wishing he wouldn't *do* that. Acting as if she had some sort of hidden agenda when she definitely didn't. Hadn't she made that clear enough last night? 'I'm sure Marina doesn't want me hanging around all the time. But don't let me stop you from doing your own thing. I'm perfectly happy with my own company.'

He smiled as he poured them both a coffee. 'I like it,' he said. 'Quite like old times.'

For a moment she said nothing because this was nothing like old times. She'd woken this morning feeling disorientated, aware that she'd spent the night in bed with Xenon but that he hadn't touched her. Or rather, he had. He'd touched her in a way which was completely out of character. He'd *held* her. Just held her. And it had been tender rather than sexual. More than that, he'd actually listened to her and then had gone out of his way to explain some of his more controlling behaviour.

Didn't he realise how confused that made her feel?

She shot him a quick glance. 'Phyllida also said that we can go and see your grandmother after breakfast.'

'Right.'

She saw the sudden tension which had darkened his face. 'I hope she's not in any pain.'

He shook his head. 'The doctors are very good about managing the pain these days and at least we are able to care for her here at home.' He put his cup down. 'It was last time I was here that she began asking about you. You know, she liked you, Lex. She liked you a lot.'

Lexi met his eyes, incredibly touched by his words because she had liked Xenon's *ghiaghia*, too. She hadn't known any of her own grandparents—maternal or paternal—and maybe that was why she'd enjoyed the company of the Greek matriarch so much. She'd loved hearing about her own far-off childhood here on this island and her long and subsequently happy marriage. 'What did she say?'

He looked at her with the expression of a man weighing up his options. 'She said that I was a very clever man, but that sometimes I could be a fool. And that I was a fool to let you go.'

'Xenon.' Her voice rose with sudden anxiety. 'I don't want to lie to her.'

'I'm not asking you to. But do you think you could manage to do a convincing enough impression of still caring for me?'

She met his gaze. If only he had said it with his habitual arrogance—an attitude which sprang from the certain knowledge that pretty much every woman he met cared about him. But he hadn't said it in that way. For a minute back then he'd sounded almost vulnerable.

Her untouched peach seemed to stare balefully at her from the plate. Maybe he *was* feeling vulnerable— or as close to it as someone like him could get to such an emotion. His beloved grandmother was dying and Lexi knew she had to stand by him. She owed him her support at this time because she had loved him and had married him. She would be there for him.

Some impulse made her stand up and reach out her hand to run her fingers through the tangle of his ebony hair. 'Oh, I think I'm a good enough actress to put on a convincing enough performance of caring for you.' She smiled.

But something in the air had changed. Something she had said or done had clearly angered him, for he rose to his feet and suddenly he seemed *huge* as his shadow fell over her.

'Good enough actress?' he echoed. 'Is that a fact?'

Without warning, he pulled her into his arms and started to kiss her and it was as if someone had opened a floodgate. His lips were hard on hers as he explored her mouth with an urgent kind of hunger. The man who had lain so chastely beside her during the night had gone and in his place was the Xenon she remembered best.

He pressed his body closer. She could feel the jut of his hips against hers and the heavy weight of his erection pressing into her belly. She could feel the insistent tug of desire melting insistently at her core—a hot ache which was clamouring to be released. His hand cupped her breast and she groaned, wriggling luxuriously as he played with one peaking nipple. Restlessly, she moved her hips in silent invitation. Wanting him to slide his hand up underneath her dress to where she was wet and waiting. Wondering if she dared touch *him*. To stroke him as he loved to be stroked. To take the heavy weight of him in her hand and to whisper her fingertips over his silken length until he moaned something guttural in his native tongue in response. Yet something stopped her from initiating that next step towards total intimacy— for wouldn't he interpret such a move as weakness or reliance on him?

So why didn't *he* make a move instead? Why didn't he push her back inside the villa and slide her onto the cool marble floor and take her without further ceremony in that hungry macho way of his? If he'd straddled her right there and then, she would have eagerly welcomed him into her body because she wanted him so badly it felt almost like pain.

But he didn't do that. Instead he drew his head away from hers, although his blue eyes were almost black with lust. And although she could see the faint tremble of his hands, his voice was quite calm when he spoke.

'I must say, Lex,' he observed, 'that you put on a pretty convincing performance of "caring for me"—even without the benefit of an audience. Don't you think?'

And Lexi knew she'd walked into a trap of her own making. A stupid and cheapening trap. She'd shown him she still wanted him and that was bad enough—but she prayed that he wouldn't guess the real reason behind her passionate response to him.

That she was still in total thrall to her husband.

'Fifteen-love,' she said.

'I'd say it was closer to set point.' His voice was dry. 'Come on, let's go and see *Ghiaghia*.'

She asked for five minutes to compose herself, to tidy her hair and smooth down her dress, and was quiet as they walked across the courtyard to the side of the house where they'd eaten dinner last night. Her heart was in her mouth as they walked into the large bedroom whose shutters were half closed and where his grandmother now lay.

Sometimes Lexi was grateful that she hadn't had a sheltered upbringing and this was one of them. As a child she had seen things no child should ever see—shocking, brutal things—but she found herself thinking that nothing was more shocking than the inevitable approach of death.

Like her daughter, Sofia had once been a great beauty but her exquisite bones were now cruelly defined by the waxy skin stretched tightly over them. Her once-lustrous eyes were dulled by morphine and her body was as insubstantial as a sparrow's as it lay beneath the white sheet.

Her eyes tried to focus on the couple as they walked into the room and for a moment she frowned, as if she was examining her failing memory for clues. But then came the hint of a smile as she stared at Lexi. The faintest fluttering of bony fingers as she attempted to lift her hand from the bed in greeting.

Lexi went straight over to her, wanting to hug her tightly but, mindful of her frailty, she bent down and took her hand before bending to kiss each shrunken cheek.

'*Ghiaghia,*' she whispered. 'It's me, Alexi.'

'Alexi.' The Greek matriarch struggled a little and Lexi glanced over at the nurse, who nodded, and the two women helped move the old lady further up the bed, positioning her feeble body against a deep pile of pillows. 'I am happy to see you.'

'And I you. Oh, *Ghiaghia.*' Lexi's voice cracked, just a little. 'I'm…I'm so sorry that you're sick.'

For a moment, Sofia looked into her eyes and there was a trace of humour on her face as well as sadness. 'It happens to us all,' she said gently.

'Yes.' Still holding onto the old lady's hand, Lexi sat

down on the chair beside the bed. 'Can I get you any-thing? Can I do anything for you?'

There was a pause and then a croak as Sofia sucked in a breath. 'Love my grandson,' she said, on the out-breath. 'As he loves you.'

For a moment Lexi felt scared. She was here because Xenon had wanted her to be and she could see exactly why. Sofia had obviously wanted to say what was on her mind and no words were more powerful than those spoken on the deathbed.

But she was also aware that she could not tell a lie—not even at a time like this. Yet the stupidest thing was that she had no *need* to lie. That what she was about to say came straight from the heart. She was grateful that Xenon was standing on the other side of the room and could not hear their whispered exchange as she bent her head to speak. 'I love Xenon more than I have ever loved any man, *Ghiaghia*,' she said. 'Please know that.'

For a moment there was silence and Lexi was left wondering if Sofia had actually heard her, or whether she had fallen asleep. But then the fingers which she was holding gripped hers with a sudden fierce show of strength and Lexi saw her smile.

The old lady's breathing grew shallow—and then she *did* fall asleep, though Lexi didn't move from her place by the bed. For a long time she sat there in silence as thoughts flew through her mind. She thought of Sofia as a young bride, and then a mother. She thought how quickly a life could pass. She was barely aware that

Xenon had walked from the far side of the room to stand behind her and had put his hand on her shoulder.

'Come on,' he said.

His voice was gentle and so was the hand which helped lever her to her feet. He moved to take her place by the bed and leaned over to kiss his grandmother tenderly on the forehead. And Lexi could feel a terrible, aching sadness.

Outside the day seemed bright—almost too bright—and the intense beauty provided an exquisite contrast to what she had just witnessed. She stood there, unsure what to do next, and when Xenon stood behind her and wrapped his arms around her, she didn't have the strength to oppose him. She leaned against him, breathing in his distinctive scent and allowing some of his strength to flow into her.

She didn't know how long they stood like that—maybe only for a couple of minutes, but when she tried to pull away he turned her round so that she was facing him and his blue eyes looked very bright.

'Thank you,' he said.

'I was glad to do it. She is a remarkable woman.'

But she found herself thinking that he was showing emotion—real emotion. And some lingering sense of resentment began to bubble up inside her. Because he hadn't shown emotion over their baby, had he?

'Lex?'

She swallowed. She couldn't go back and she couldn't keep blaming him for the way he'd been. She guessed he had coped in the way only he knew how to cope, as had she. It was just that they hadn't managed to cope together.

'Lex?' he said again. 'We need to think about how we're going to spend our day and you look like you could use a little sun on your face. How about a trip around the island?' A dry, teasing note entered his voice. 'Maybe take the bike out?'

She looked at him suspiciously. 'You're not still riding that clapped-out old motorbike?'

'Actually no, I have a new one. All gleaming black and chrome and much more comfortable than the last. It's the only way to travel.'

'Thankfully, it's not.'

'Oh, come on—you know you always secretly liked riding pillion.'

She met the mockery in his eyes and told herself this was dangerous. That a sensible person would change into a bikini and take a book down to the pool and maybe spend the rest of the day reading. But then she thought about Sofia. She thought about an island she had missed and a beautiful day which might never come again.

'Okay,' she said. 'Why not?'

CHAPTER EIGHT

IT WAS A long time since Lexi had been on the back of a motorbike. Not since her last visit here, just before she'd become pregnant. Before the pressure had become so intense and they'd started to treat her as if she had been made of porcelain. When she'd been made so aware of the significance of the child she carried...

Squashing the helmet over her ponytailed hair, she wriggled onto the pillion seat behind him.

'Where do you want to go?' he threw over his shoulder.

'Surprise me.'

'Okay.' He kick-started the bike and it pulled away with a throaty roar as the electronic gates swung open.

They headed off down the road, with dust billowing up in clouds as they passed and Lexi felt the first heady rush of freedom as they headed down the hillside.

She noticed that he avoided the busy coastal road and wondered if he might take her to the famous Acropolis of Lindos, with its Knights' stairway and view over St Paul's bay, which was considered one of the most stunning in all Greece. But that would have been an unwelcome surprise because it was the place where he'd asked her to marry him, during an unforgettable day of high romance and promise. And an overwhelming sense of relief washed over her when he headed inland, through the tiny hillside village of Laerma and then out onto the Profila road.

Xenon's new bike was powerful, but Lexi realised that he must have remembered her fear of high speed, because he quashed his dare-devil nature and took it at a relatively easy pace. Which meant that she was able to enjoy the breathtaking views of an island which the ancient Greeks had described as 'more beautiful than the sun'.

The only trouble with motorbikes, she reflected, was that you had to get close. Like, really close. As a passenger you had to grip the waist of the person in front and cling to them like glue. She was being given a legitimate reason to touch her husband and she couldn't decide if it was heaven or hell.

Her senses felt as if they were being assaulted from all sides. The beauty of the island and the sense of freedom which warmed her skin as she hung onto Xenon was heady stuff. And she wasn't naïve enough to deny that the throb of the powerful machine between her legs was making her think about things she definitely shouldn't be thinking about.

They drove for about twenty miles before he brought the bike to a halt on the dusty road close to the monastery of Moni Thari and turned his head to look at her. 'Do you want to stop and go inside?'

She'd been here before, too. In fact, Lexi realised that there were few places on the island she hadn't visited, but today it seemed appropriate to go inside that spiritual place and to think of Sofia.

'I'd like that.'

He parked close to the monastery and they went inside. The thickness of the ancient walls meant that the interior was cool and welcoming and the echoing silence seemed to seep into her skin and fill her with a strange sense of calm.

But as they paused to study the exquisite frescoes, Lexi felt as if she was being emotionally tugged in all directions. She was acutely aware of Xenon at her side, his motorcycle helmet tucked beneath his arm. With his dark hair ruffled and windswept, he looked dressed-down and casual. But no matter what he wore or how he presented himself, he always drew the eye.

She could see a couple of beautiful Swedish women turning to stare at him and she saw the expressions on their faces. And it was always like that. Women always looked at him and wanted him. Yet there was nothing to suggest that the man studying the frescoes with such rapt curiosity was a powerful billionaire with global influence. He just looked so very *Greek*.

Afterwards, he drove them back to Laerma, only this time they stopped for a drink in the little village. Under the dappled shadows of the trees, they sat outside a small restaurant whose owner came out to greet Xenon, shaking his hand enthusiastically, as if he was an old friend.

It appeared he was, because Xenon introduced him to Lexi as Petros. He served them with thick coffee, water and a plate of salty olives and went inside, only to reappear a few minutes later holding a small plastic bag, which he handed to Xenon.

'*Efharisto,*' said Xenon, inclining his head slightly as he glanced inside.

'*Parakalo.*' Petros gave him a questioning look. '*Ine simantiko?*'

'*Ne.*'

Lexi waited until they'd finished their drinks and were walking back towards the bike before she brought the subject up.

'What was Petros saying to you?'

'He was asking me whether something was important.'

She scurried to keep up with his long stride. 'And you said it was?'

He smiled. 'Very good, Lex. You now know the word for "yes". Your Greek is improving.'

'Very funny. Does it have something to do with that plastic bag?'

'It does.'

'What's in it?'

He patted the back pocket of his jeans. 'A film.'

'Is that all you're going to tell me?'

He flicked her a glance, tempted to remind her that she was no longer his wife and therefore she should not expect a wife's privileges. But her silvery-green eyes looked so earnest that he found himself capitulating.

'I'm surprised you hadn't worked it out for yourself. Remember those photos taken of us outside the jeweller's?' He gave a hard smile of triumph. 'Well, this is the rogue film.'

Lexi blinked. 'You mean you got it back?'

'Of course. I told you that I'd sorted it. You were obviously upset at the thought of the images getting out, so I spoke to Petros and he arranged for one of his sons to…retrieve it.'

She remembered the brief telephone conversation he'd had in the car. The sense of power which had shimmered from his dark and brooding frame as he had barked out his instructions. 'And the photographer handed them over—just like that?'

'Something like that.' Xenon gave the ghost of a smile. 'What is it they say? That I made him an offer he couldn't refuse.'

Lexi's teeth bit into her bottom lip. She tried telling herself that his behaviour was high-handed and that he was a complete control freak. Yet she couldn't deny her gratitude to him, because those photos could have come back to haunt her. When she went back to Devon, the last thing she wanted was to have to face renewed speculation about her relationship with Xenon. And if she was being brutally honest with herself, didn't his power and authority sometimes *thrill* her?

Didn't she sometimes fight him for the sake of fighting him? Because maybe another of her default mechanisms was that she simply wasn't used to a man who wanted to protect her.

'Thank you,' she said carefully.

'*Parakalo,*' he answered with equal care, his eyes mocking her. 'At least now you needn't fear any new photographic evidence linking us.'

'You must have read my mind!'

'I must have done.'

But Xenon recognised that the light-hearted interlude was masking a growing tension between them. He could feel his body growing uncomfortably hard the longer he was alone with her. He could feel her arms snaking around him as she climbed onto the bike. In his driving mirror he could see the flash of her bare thighs. Briefly, he closed his eyes because her breasts were pushed against him as they moved away and he thought that this was pretty close to torture.

If it had been anyone other than Lexi, he would have stopped on the way back at one of the many secluded settings through which they passed. He would have parked the bike where it could not be seen from the road and then taken her in his arms and tumbled her down onto the ground. There would be no time to remove her dress and, besides, that pale, sensitive flesh of hers might be damaged by pine needles digging into her back. He swallowed. There would be no time for anything other than to slide her panties off and to lose himself inside her tight, liquid heat again.

The fantasy became so intense that the bike swerved a little as he imagined that first, sweet moment of entry.

'For God's sake, Xenon!'

The angry rush of her words in his ear brought him

to his senses and he slowed right down. 'What's the matter?'

'You're driving like a maniac!'

'I'm not used to anyone riding pillion.'

'That's no excuse. Just concentrate, will you?'

'I'll try.' How could he concentrate when she was glued to him like that? He toyed with the idea of suggesting that she didn't need to clamp her thighs around him *quite* so tightly, but realised that he was enjoying it too much to want her to stop.

The remainder of the journey was accomplished without incident and when they returned to the house it was to see Phyllida and several other women in the gardens, weaving fairy-lights into the trees. Long tables had been erected and were being decorated with thick garlands of flowers.

Xenon held out his hand to help Lexi off the bike. 'My sister is taking this christening very seriously,' he observed wryly. 'Oh and, by the way, she's bringing the baby over to meet you later. I should have mentioned it before.'

Lexi froze. It was stupid. Unpredictable. She should have been expecting something like this and yet the word was like the shock of cold water colliding with warm skin. She tried to smile but maybe her attempt was unconvincing, because he caught hold of her as she turned away.

'Lex? What is it?'

'It doesn't matter.' She shook off his hand and began to walk towards their villa but she could hear his footsteps following her and she couldn't do a damned thing to stop him. She went inside and heard the door slam shut behind him.

'For God's sake, Lex—just talk to me!'

'It's nothing.'

'It's *something*,' he said fiercely. 'How am I supposed to help when you won't tell me what's wrong?'

She stared at him for a moment, gathering her breath and wishing that her heart wasn't beating so fiercely. 'You can't "help" me,' she said fiercely. 'Nobody can.'

'Is it because I mentioned the baby?'

'What do you think?' she questioned as all the feelings she'd bottled up for so long came spilling out in a dark and unstoppable tide. 'Don't you ever think what he might be like now? Our little boy? He'd be two years old, Xenon. Imagine that. Running around with dark hair and blue eyes just like his daddy. Stumbling over a little plastic ball in the courtyard—'

'Stop it!' he said, in a strangled kind of voice.

'But you asked me,' she said. 'And I'm telling you. I'm telling you what it's like. It hardly happens at all these days, but it was there all the time at the beginning. The pain and the loss. The rewriting of a future into something you don't recognise. Do you want to know what it was like, Xenon—I mean, do you *really*?'

He thought that he'd never seen her like this before. He'd never seen her look quite so *helpless*. Because this was Lexi. Lexi, who had always been so strong. Like him, she'd had to be. Maybe even stronger than him because all the odds had been stacked up against her, right from the start. He nodded, but behind his lips his teeth were clenched. 'Tell me,' he ground out.

The words came stumbling over themselves. 'Every pram that passed me in the street was like an arrow to the heart. You remember all those cute little baby outfits I bought?' She sucked in a ragged breath. 'Well, they just seemed to taunt me with what we could never have. Taking them down to the charity shop was so… *heartbreaking*.'

'You could have kept them,' he said. 'We could have tried again for another baby.'

She flinched and shook her head. 'And how was that going to happen—when you wouldn't come near me afterwards? You couldn't even bear to touch me, because I'd failed. I'd failed to provide a son and heir for the continuation of the Kanellis dynasty!'

He groped for the right response, but he who was so fluent could find no words in his vocabulary suitable for what he wanted to say. 'I couldn't—'

'You couldn't bear to touch me,' she repeated. 'And that's the truth!'

'Because I didn't know how to comfort you,' he said. 'I didn't know what to say. I'm still having difficulty saying it now.'

His obvious remorse stabbed at her heart. It made her want to comfort him, but Lexi knew that she couldn't afford to crumble. For both their sakes she had to face facts.

'Then let me say it for you. The first time I miscarried, I was only a few weeks gone and I hadn't had much of a chance to get used to it. But the second time I was nineteen weeks pregnant. In some countries, that's only a week away from what is termed as a stillbirth, Xenon, and that is something which people take seriously. But nobody seemed to take this seriously. It was the hardest and biggest thing I've ever had to go through and yet I felt as if everyone wanted to forget about my baby. To act like nothing had happened.'

He felt as if someone had driven a stake deep inside his heart. His hands were trembling as he stared at her. 'Oh, God, Lex.'

She shook her head, trying to blot out the look on his face because somehow his bleak compassion was only making it a million times worse. 'Everyone tells you that you'll get over it. That you can go out and "have another one". As if it's a coat that you left on the train which you can replace by going shopping.'

The silence which followed was broken only by the sound of her breathing.

'Why didn't you tell me you felt like this?' he demanded. 'Why the hell didn't you talk to me about it at the time?'

'And when was I supposed to do that?' she said. 'You threw yourself into your work as if it was the only thing which mattered and moved into one of the other bedrooms. It was achingly obvious that your disappointment was so great, you could hardly bear to look at me.'

He saw for the first time how she must have interpreted his behaviour. That his inability to deal with his own feelings had helped create the vast chasm which had grown between them.

'I *was* disappointed,' he said heavily. 'I cannot deny that. I guess that was my way of coping—the only way I knew. I was aware that I needed to be strong for you—but how could I do that if you could see that inside my heart was breaking, too?'

Her lips buckled as she stared at him, because that was the saddest thing he'd ever said. And never had she felt the pain of their parting so profoundly—nor been swamped by such a yearning wish that it could all have been different. She felt a sob rise up in her throat like a wave whipped up during a high storm.

'Oh, Xenon,' she said, her voice breaking.

She saw his jaw clench. Saw him shake his head before he pulled her into his arms and started to kiss her in the most raw and savage way imaginable. His mouth came down to crush against hers and she felt the heat of his hunger. Opening her lips beneath that first fierce onslaught, she clung to him and kissed him back. He was cupping her face like a man possessed, as if he couldn't get enough of her, and somehow her glasses had slipped off. She heard them clatter onto the floor. But Lexi didn't care. She didn't care about anything because now he was backing her into the bedroom, still kissing her and she could scarcely breathe as he tore his mouth away from hers, and pushed her down onto the bed.

She guessed he was giving her time to change her mind. Why else would he stand there, slowly unbuckling his belt, his eyes not leaving hers? He peeled off his white T-shirt and briefly closed his eyes before easing his zip down. She heard him kicking off his shoes and the rustle as his jeans and boxers followed.

Suddenly he was completely naked and he came towards the bed and straddled her. 'Lex,' he said.

She could feel the hardness of his thighs as he leaned over and brushed his mouth over hers. She could see how aroused he was but he seemed hell-bent on demonstrating his self-control as he began to unbutton her dress. She squirmed as each button popped free and the cool air hit her skin. She saw the darkening of his eyes as he caught his first sight of her bra and knickers and she couldn't hold back any longer. Reaching out, she caught his erection in her hand, gasping in a shocked breath as her fingers closed round him. It had been so long since she'd touched him. So long since she'd seen him naked like this.

'Turn over,' he said roughly. 'And let me get this damned dress off.'

Had she thought that he'd been demonstrating self-control? Because suddenly it seemed to have deserted him as he peeled the dress from her body with shaking hands and threw it onto the ground. Her bra and panties followed, until she was as naked as he was.

And then she remembered.

How the hell could she have forgotten?

'I'm not on the pill,' she said.

His face darkened. 'And why would you be, when

we have not been sleeping together?' he demanded arrogantly.

'Because we haven't been *living* together! We're separated!'

'But you are still my wife, Lex. *You are still my wife!*'

With a muttered curse he walked over to the closet and opened one of the drawers until he had found what he was looking for.

She watched as he tore open the foil, and as all their tumultuous history crowded into her mind Lexi thought maybe she should call a halt to this madness. But any remaining reason was soon silenced by desire. Her throat dried as she watched him stroking on the condom and it was much too late for a change of heart, because he was walking back towards the bed and the look on his face was making her melt with longing.

He returned to his previous position on the bed, with one thigh on either side of her. He bent his head and grazed his mouth over her nipples, teasing each tip into an exquisitely sensitised bud. Her hands flew to his head, her nails digging into his scalp as she lifted her hips towards his in wordless plea.

He slid his fingers down between her thighs, murmuring something indistinct when he felt just how wet she was. But Lexi saw the convulsive way he swallowed, as if he had a lump the size of a golf ball stuck in his throat. And that one small chink of vulnerability made her wrap her arms tightly around his neck.

'Xenon,' she breathed.

'Lex,' he gasped. 'Oh, Lex.'

She moaned against his neck as he reached down to brush the tip of his erection against her waiting heat.

And never had anything seemed so symbolic as that first deep thrust, though he stilled when she cried out his name in a broken kind of way.

'I am hurting you?' he demanded.

'No,' she whispered. 'It's beautiful. Just beautiful.'

Her heartfelt words stirred him more than he would have anticipated, but then it had been a long time since he'd heard such tenderness in her voice. It wrapped itself around his heart like a velvet fist as he made love to her as if it were the very first time. It felt like sweet and exquisite torture as he tried not to come too quickly— when he wanted to come as soon as he'd entered her. He tried to think of other things. But he couldn't.

Suddenly he was at the mercy of feelings so powerful that he almost lost control—he, who had never lost control in his life. Suddenly his head was bent and he was kissing her as if that kiss were the only thing sustaining him, as if it were as necessary to him as the very air which he breathed.

Her soft, pale thighs were tight around his back and he was lifting her up towards him, so that she was pinned almost effortlessly against his body while he thrust deep inside her.

He saw her head tip back just before that first low cry came from her lips. A sound once so familiar yet now so strange that he could have wept.

But then his own orgasm came to his rescue. It exploded like a truckload of dark fireworks going off in slow motion, before wrapping him in oblivion. And the last thing he could remember saying was her name.

CHAPTER NINE

FOR A MOMENT Lexi wondered why she felt so strange.

There was warmth and weight and an odd, aching feeling.

And a sound.

Her eyes fluttered open to see Xenon fast asleep beside her. The bed was huge but he was managing to take up most of it with his long limbs sprawled languidly over the ruffled sheets. Against the pristine whiteness of Egyptian cotton, his hair was as black as night and his olive skin looked like burnished gold.

She realised that the sound she'd heard had been his breathing—steady and slow—and the weight was one hair-roughened thigh imprisoning her own pale leg beneath. And the aching? She felt the sudden rush of colour flooding into her cheeks as she remembered.

Xenon making love to her.

Xenon lifting her up as if she'd been weightless and thrusting into her.

Xenon pinning her against the wall on her way back from retrieving her glasses from the sitting-room floor. A kiss which had turned into something more. She remembered the cool wall pressing against her back and one very hot, aroused man at her front.

She turned her head to stare at the blurred outline of the ceiling light, knowing that if she reached out for her glasses she might wake him. And she didn't want to wake him; she badly needed a moment to be alone with her thoughts.

She closed her eyes. It had been amazing. It always was. He'd made her feel as if she'd come alive—properly alive. As if her body had been designed for Xenon to make love to her. As if she'd been empty without him.

But nothing had changed, she reminded herself. She mustn't make the classic female mistake of thinking that an afternoon of incredible sex was going to make any real difference to them.

'Kiss me.'

His murmured entreaty broke into the silence and Lexi stilled, not knowing how to react to him after what had happened. Clearly unwilling to wait, he reached out a strong hand and imprisoned her, locking his arm tightly around her waist as he levered her close so that she was confronted by the gleam of a pair of bright blue eyes.

The eyes narrowed and his lips curved. 'I said, kiss me.'

'Is that an order?'

'Would you like it to be?'

Reluctantly, Lexi felt her own smile tug back. How could you stop yourself from doing something you really wanted even though you knew it was probably wrong? She leaned forward and drifted her mouth over his. 'You're incorrigible.'

His hand moved from her waist to her bare bottom. 'Is that a good thing, or a bad thing?'

'I can't decide.' The temptation to continue flirting was close to irresistible, but Lexi forced herself to remember what was happening in the world outside this bedroom. The household would be gearing up for tomorrow's christening and later today she was going to meet the baby who was still theoretically her niece. It wasn't going to be an easy situation given her wobbly emotions around babies and especially now that she had complicated matters by having sex with Xenon.

But this wasn't about her and what had happened in the past. It was about Kyra and her family and Xenon's beloved grandmother.

She grabbed her glasses from the bedside table and turned to him. 'Do you think I should offer to help with the christening preparations?'

'I suspect that my mother probably has everything in hand. And since a lot of the tradespeople will be speaking Greek and your vocabulary is still in single figures, it's probably best…' he traced a finger from neck to breastbone, where he spread his hand out wide so that his fingers brushed against both her peaking nipples '…if you use your time more constructively by devoting it to me.'

This is what he does, she told herself as she felt her body responding to his touch. *He fashions the world to suit his needs. And he does so by making you want him—even though you know you shouldn't.* She gave a half-hearted wriggle.

'I need to shower and change before your sister arrives.'

He cupped her breast, and bent his head to kiss it. 'Anyone would think you were running away.'

'I need a shower,' she repeated stubbornly, even though his tongue was cleaving a delectable path over the puckering nub.

He looked up from her breast. 'You don't think we need to talk about what's just happened?'

'And what *has* just happened? We had sex. It was good sex…' She saw the look on his face. 'No, amend that. It was great sex. It always is. You don't need me to tell you that, Xenon. But it doesn't change anything.'

'On the contrary—I think it changes everything.' He pushed a spill of hair away from her face. 'And it's not just "great sex"—if it were that simple then don't you think I might have found it elsewhere?'

'Oh, I see.' She gave a short laugh. 'So suddenly this has become a boastful testimony about your general irresistibility to women?'

'I wouldn't know about that.' He coiled a strand of hair around his finger. 'Because since the moment I met you, you've been the only woman I've ever wanted.'

She looked at him warily. 'You mean…you haven't been to bed with anyone else?'

'No, I haven't been to bed with anyone else,' he growled. 'I haven't wanted to and I took my marriage vows seriously when I made them. I thought you did, too.'

'I *did*,' she said in a small voice, but now she was left wondering whether she had really believed in them. Hadn't she felt a sense of disbelief that someone like Xenon should want someone like her?

Because beneath all the outward trappings of being a famous pop-star, she had always felt like the insecure outsider who nobody would really want. The girl in glasses who'd been laughed at whenever she'd actually made it into school. The girl with the shabby second-hand clothes and the promiscuous mother. Her view of life had been warped by her experience and she guessed that had been inevitable. She had never seen a relationship which worked and she had certainly never seen one which lasted. Was it any wonder that she'd had no idea about how to proceed with her own marriage?

She had tried to accept Xenon's overwhelming control of their lives—her life—as something normal within a marriage. But she hadn't really known what 'normal' was. She remembered how eager she'd been to please. How terrified she'd been of doing the wrong thing. Like a tightrope walker, she had stuck to the route he'd set out for her, never daring to deviate nor to look down in case she might fall.

And by doing that, hadn't she made herself yet another responsibility to add to the load already pressing down on his shoulders?

'I tried as hard as I could to make it work,' she said. 'But I can see now that I allowed myself to become completely dominated by the force of your personality and your power. And that wasn't fair—not to either of us.'

'We should have talked about it.'

'But it's impossible to communicate with somebody who's never there.'

Their eyes met and when he spoke his voice was grave. 'So what if I tell you that I recognise I wasn't there for you? Not just when you lost the baby but afterwards. And maybe some time before that, too.' He saw the way she flinched. 'And what If I told you that I will ensure that never happens again? That I will learn to accept the things over which I have no control—what then, Lex? Are you really willing to just give up on all the good things which still exist between us? The compatibility and the chemistry and the...' His blue eyes blazed a slow trail over her face. 'The unbelievable *fire*.'

For a moment Lexi didn't answer. Her mind was buzzing as she tried to find the right response. He was so clever with words and she was not. Years of negotiating at the top end of the business world had guaranteed him the slick gift of persuasion. He could probably sell hot chocolate on a baking hot beach and convince people it was the next best thing.

But how much of his declaration was about his wounded pride—about the fact that *she* had been the one who had walked out? For a man of Xenon's standing, that would not have looked good. He'd told her that he'd never failed at anything. Wasn't it possible that his suggestion they give their relationship another go was simply being driven by his ego?

Deep down she doubted whether he could ever be the kind of man who would just *accept* things. How would that work when for him control came as easily as breathing?

She shook her head. 'It's not a question of "giving up" but more a case of letting go. Too much has happened.' Now she could feel the light trail of his thumb against her pulse. Could he tell how frantically it was beating? Did he know that she was having the fight of her life against her own desires? 'I'm not the right kind of woman for you.'

'You don't think that I should be the one to decide that?'

'Let's just say I'm helping you out.' She lowered her voice to a whisper. 'You only want me because you can't have me.'

'No, Lex. I want you because I want you.'

Lexi met the unyielding expression in his eyes as a silent tussle of wills took place. But she had learnt plenty from her time living with him—and she knew that fighting him was no good. It never had been any good, because he always had to win. So why not meet him halfway? There was nothing wrong with indulging their physical needs while she was here, even if their other needs could never be met. Sooner or later it was inevitable that Xenon would come to the same conclusion as her and, until he did, why not just enjoy the chemistry he'd spoken of? She brushed her fingers over his lips.

'Enough of the heavy stuff. Come on, Xenon—think

about your sister and baby Ianthe's special day. Isn't that why we're here? Hmm?' She dodged the kiss he aimed at her lips. 'So I am going to take a shower and I don't care what you say—because you are *not* going to change my mind!'

He found himself laughing as he watched her get up from the bed with a grace which had once transfixed concert-goers the world over—himself included. Except that none of her fans would have recognised the woman who was heading for the bathroom. He thought how unselfconsciously beautiful she looked, naked but for that geeky pair of glasses, her strawberry-blonde hair cascading down to her waist.

He shook his head in bemusement because she was frustrating the hell out of him, but, when he stopped to think about it, hadn't she always done that? She was unpredictable. As slippery as an eel. He had just made love to her but afterwards he had sensed those damned barriers going up again.

He headed for the second bathroom and turned the shower on cold, shivering as the icy rivulets coursed over his heated flesh. This was getting to be a habit, he thought grimly as he rubbed shampoo into his hair.

Afterwards, he went back into the bedroom to find Lexi already dressed. She was sitting at the dressing-table mirror and putting on mascara in front of some sort of magnifying mirror.

He pulled a fresh shirt from the wardrobe, wondering how she could she sit there looking so damned *composed*—as if nothing had happened. Dropping the towel, which was the only thing between him and nakedness, he saw her flickering glance reflected back at him in the mirror. He saw the faint flush which stained her cheeks and he smiled. Nice to know that she wasn't completely immune to him.

'Want to come over here and button up my shirt for me?' he drawled.

'You're a big boy now, Xenon—I think you can probably manage on your own.'

But he noticed that the hand which replaced the mascara wand was trembling a little and he felt a disproportionate sense of triumph.

Kyra arrived soon afterwards, accompanied by her husband, Nikola, who was carrying their baby daughter, Ianthe. Lexi stared at Xenon's pretty sister and her mouth broke into a wide smile.

'Lexi!' squealed Kyra, running across the courtyard and throwing her arms around her. 'I can't believe you're actually here—or that you've stopped dyeing your hair!'

'Nice to see you, too!' laughed Lexi.

She hugged the younger woman tightly and was introduced to her rather serious-faced husband, Nikola. But Lexi knew she couldn't keep putting off the inevitable and at last she turned her attention to Ianthe. The baby was plump and apple-cheeked, her features shaded beneath a silky bonnet designed to protect her delicate head from the sun.

Lexi could feel the stab of pain as she stared down at the button nose. She thought she could see a trace of

Xenon's mouth in the rosebud shape of her mouth—or was that just wishful thinking? She stroked one soft little cheek and felt a wave of longing washing over her as she looked down at the little girl.

'Oh, Kyra, she's beautiful.'

'Isn't she?' Kyra beamed, her blue eyes glowing. 'Well, I'm her mother so of course I'm biased, but Nikola agrees with me that she is the most beautiful baby in the world. And she sleeps. Oh, how she sleeps! Sometimes we can't believe our luck, can we, darling? Oh look, here's *Mitera*.'

Lexi looked across the courtyard to see Marina Kanellis walking towards them, unruffled and cool in a dress of pale linen. She kissed her daughter and son-in-law and then held out her arms for the baby, before raising her brows at Lexi.

'That is unless you would like to hold her, Alexi?'

'Yes, Lexi, hold her,' urged Kyra.

Lexi held her breath and for one crazy moment it felt as if they were all looking at her and *judging* her. As if they were all conspiring in some secret experiment to see how much she would be affected by the presence of the baby. Xenon's blue gaze seemed to be lancing through her and she wondered if her face was showing the irrational fear she felt inside.

But maybe this was what she needed to do. She couldn't go through the rest of her life shying away from one of the most essential parts of it and babies *were* an essential part. Her brothers might go on to have families of their own—she certainly hoped so—and she would want to be a part of those families.

Tentatively, she nodded. 'I'm not very good with babies.'

'Oh, you'll soon learn!' said Kyra as Nikola put the little bundle in her arms.

Lexi held the baby close and breathed in her sweet, warm scent. She felt the weight of her small but surprisingly substantial body and hugged her closer.

'See!' said Kyra, with a note of triumph. 'You're a natural. You'll make a great mother yourself one day, Lexi.'

Lexi couldn't speak. For a moment she could scarcely breathe. Had they forgotten, or had they just chosen to forget? She wanted to say that she *was* a mother—and nobody could ever take that away from her. Just because her baby hadn't lived, didn't mean that she hadn't once carried Xenon's child, did it?

And then, to her horror, the infant turned her head, instinctively rooting around as her little mouth searched fruitlessly for Lexi's breast. Despite the temperature, she stood frozen to the spot, hoping that the heat of the day hid her blush. 'I think she may be hungry.'

Kyra was giggling as she plucked her daughter from Lexi's arms. 'She's always hungry! Why don't you and I go inside while I feed her? You can tell me all about your jewellery business and I might even commission a couple of pieces, since Xenon says they're very good.'

Lexi looked up, to find Xenon's gaze still on her,

glad for the swift change of subject. 'Did you?' she asked, in surprise.

'Well, the investor in me has always preferred gold to silver,' he admitted, his gaze drifting to the amethyst-studded coils of silver which were dangling from her ears. 'But I can see for myself that they are very beautiful.'

His unexpected compliment went a little way towards soothing Lexi's ruffled nerves, but the prospect of watching his sister feed the baby was an ordeal she would rather have foregone. Nonetheless, she followed Kyra into the grand house and perched on the edge of one of the sofas. She watched as the baby was latched onto her mother's breast and Kyra settled back with a contented little sigh, before turning a quizzical blue gaze on her.

'So you're back?' she said, without preamble. 'Back with my brother—my darling brother—and I can't tell you how happy that makes me. You know, even my mother is pleased?'

Lexi hesitated and for a moment she longed to slip into the role which seemed to have been created for her. Suddenly she wanted to be Xenon's wife again, in every way that counted. But if she allowed herself to believe the fantasy—even for a second—it would make walking away all the harder. 'I'm only here for the christening,' she said.

Kyra's eyes narrowed. 'But no longer?'

'I'm afraid not.'

There was a pause, a silence during which the only

sound Lexi could hear was that of the baby glugging contentedly and as a background noise it couldn't have been more poignant. *If that had been me, then would it all have been different?* she wondered. *If I had carried Xenon's baby to term, then might the split never have happened?* But she still would have been lonely in the marriage, wouldn't she? She would still be having to fight for every second of her husband's time. She would still have been that insecure woman who was too scared to be herself.

'Lexi?'

Lexi saw Kyra screw up her face in the way people did when they weren't sure whether what they were about to say was wise.

'What?' Lexi asked softly, but she guessed what was coming next. Because she knew that Xenon's little sister had always seen the world as one great big rose-tinted ball of romance. Hadn't she gazed at her and Xenon with rapturous joy as they had taken their vows, her pink coronet of bridesmaid flowers contrasted against her gleaming dark hair?

'Xenon has missed you, Lexi. He's missed you a lot.'

'I don't want to talk about Xenon,' said Lexi gently. 'And I don't think it's appropriate to talk about him with you—much as I adore you.'

'You know, I've never seen him like that before,' Kyra said, blithely continuing as if no objection had been raised.

'Like what?' asked Lexi, curious in spite of everything.

'Like he was…*lost*.' Kyra shrugged and the baby at her breast made a loud, sucking noise as if in protest. 'Like nothing made sense any more.'

'Describing Xenon as lost would be like describing Australia as a small island,' observed Lexi wryly. 'Xenon is strong. Stronger than anyone I've ever met. He doesn't do "lost".'

'I wonder,' said Kyra slowly, 'if that isn't just the reputation he's acquired because all his life people have relied on him. Strong Xenon. Invulnerable Xenon. Xenon who goes around picking up the pieces of other people's lives and putting them back together. Maybe it's time that somebody looked out for him for a change.'

Lexi looked down at her hands. At the band of gold which was gleaming brightly on her finger. She heard what Kyra was saying and she felt a hopeless twist of longing.

Maybe somebody should look out for Xenon, but that person could never be her.

CHAPTER TEN

NEXT MORNING, LEXI got up early while Xenon was still sleeping, leaving him sprawled out on the rumpled sheets which bore testimony to their long night of love-making. Quietly, she slid a bikini from the drawer and changed in the bathroom before going outside to the vast infinity pool which overlooked the bay.

In the milky, golden light of the early morning, the distant sea glittered like sapphires and everything looked sparkling clean and fresh. Sprinklers had been spraying the flowers overnight so that their petals were still dowsed with tiny droplets of water.

The pool was cool when she dived in but Lexi was glad for the shock to her senses. Shock was good. It brought her thoughts back to the present instead of letting them meander off into a dreamy and unrealistic future. It reminded her that this tryst with Xenon was purely temporary. Well, maybe *pure* was the wrong word, but it was definitely temporary.

He had been curiously quiet after his sister had left yesterday and had remained quiet all through dinner—politely batting away the conversational gambits of his mother and swirling his wine round in his glass, without actually drinking any of it. He had seemed preoccupied, the way he used to be whenever he had some big problem at work. Mulling things over in that clever brain of his until he had identified the exact cause of the problem and how best to deal with it.

At one point she had asked him if something was wrong and he had looked at her, his blue eyes narrowed with an expression she couldn't remember ever seeing before, and had said, 'You tell me, Lex.'

She'd felt uncomfortable then and had lapsed into silence herself and not long afterwards she had excused herself from the table and gone off to bed. And when he had followed her he had seemed reluctant to have *any* kind of conversation. Instead he had started to kiss her in a hungry, almost angry way and she couldn't prevent herself from kissing him back and after that it had just rocketed out of control.

But now she couldn't get that kiss out of her mind, or the explosive love-making which had followed. And she needed to. She needed to forget the slide of his fingers on her flesh and the way his lips sought out her most sensitive places. She remembered the way his head had burrowed in between her thighs last night. She'd put her hand on his hair to stop him because at that moment it had seemed almost too intimate an act, especially when she was trying to distance herself from him.

But he hadn't stopped. He had just moved his tongue all the way along the trembling skin of her inner thigh and she had let him. He had ignored her little gasp of outraged pleasure when his lips first located that hot and aching little bud. He'd pretended he hadn't heard her muffled question about whether this was such a good idea. And then she had fallen back against the bed, her thighs parting wide and her fingers clutching at him greedily as she soared up into an intense orgasm which left her body racked with exquisite spasms.

How did he *do* that? she wondered. Dominating her so utterly and completely and turning her into both a compliant and active lover. She thought how easy it had been to slip back into the physical compatibility which had always been a huge part of their marriage. Yet when she stopped to think about it, even that side of their relationship had never really been equal. He had come to the marriage with an encyclopaedic knowledge of the opposite sex while hers could have been written on the back of a postage stamp. He was the only man she'd ever been intimate with and that had pleased him far more than it should have done. She knew that because he'd told her, in that unashamedly boastful Greek way of his.

She'd once asked him if he would have married her if she hadn't been a virgin and there had been a momentary hesitation before he had reassured her that, yes, of course he would. But Lexi had never really been convinced by that reassurance. Her virginity was all tied in with Xenon's desire for a wife-on-a-pedestal. The textbook partner for a fundamentally old-fashioned man.

And she was not that wife. She could never be that wife.

Diving beneath the surface of the pool, she opened

her eyes to the bleached blue light as she swam almost an entire length underwater before emerging, spluttering, into the fresh air.

She wondered what would lie ahead when she left here, with Jason's debts paid off and her whole life in front of her. She had her career and her home, but no emotional security. She wondered if she would ever find happiness with another man or whether she was doomed to become one of those women who always carried a torch for their first and only love. A little like Marina...

Hauling herself out of the pool, she squeezed the excess water from her hair and rubbed herself dry with a giant towel before walking back to the villa.

Xenon was standing in the doorway as she approached, a cup of coffee in hand and an inscrutable expression on his face as he watched her. Wearing nothing but a pair of faded jeans, his big body looked tense and powerful. Sunlight gleamed on the muscular arms and honed torso and Lexi was suddenly filled with an almost unbearable sense of lust. She was going to miss this. Damn it, she was going to miss *him*.

'That bikini doesn't leave much to the imagination,' he observed drily.

'You'd prefer to give your imagination something to work on, would you?'

'That depends.'

'On what?'

Broad shoulders rose and fell in a shrug but none of the tension left them. 'On what you have in mind to get it fired up.'

She looked straight into his eyes. 'How about this for starters?'

She pushed him inside and shut the door before taking his cup from him, putting it down with miraculously steady fingers. Then she put her hands onto his bare shoulders and started to kiss him.

His mouth opened instantly. He groaned as she slicked her tongue inside and began to slide it over his teeth. Her fingers moved down from his shoulders and began to explore his bare flesh. They skated lightly over his torso. She could feel the hard muscle which underpinned the silken skin and with her thumb and her forefinger she teased each of his nipples, the way he'd so often teased hers, and she heard his shuddered sigh.

'Lex—'

'Shh,' she whispered.

Downwards her fingers tiptoed, as slowly as she could make them. So slow that it was barely a move at all. She could feel him shift his body impatiently as she finally reached his belt, before moving her hand away as if she had changed her mind.

'Lex,' he moaned.

'I can't hear you.'

Xenon shut his eyes. He knew exactly what she was doing. She was playing a power game. The same game he'd been playing last night when he'd been trying to work out just what it would take to get *through* to her. Really get through to her. He swallowed. 'I'm not going to beg you.'

'That's okay.' She flicked her fingers lightly over his straining crotch. 'We're not in any hurry.'

The sustained teasing went on for several minutes before Xenon thought that he might explode. A hot rush of breath escaped from his lips and suddenly begging seemed like the best option in the world. 'Please.'

'Is this what you want?' Her hands moved down to the buckle of his belt.

'Yes. God, yes.'

'I think I'd better get these off quickly, don't you?'

'Lex—'

'Shh.'

She began to pull the zip down over his straining hardness and, carefully, her fingers freed him. She heard him groan again before she sank to her knees in front of him and the stupid thing was that the note of vulnerability in his voice just twisted at her heart. Physically, she'd never felt so in control, but emotionally she was only just hanging on by a thread as she slithered down his jeans.

He was very aroused, she thought. And so very big. She closed her eyes as his erection nudged against her cheek. Her hands splayed over his bare buttocks and she pressed her mouth against his hardness, her tongue licking a feather-light trail as it whispered down over his steely shaft.

'Lex,' he groaned, his hands clutching the side of her head as she took him deep into her mouth.

She cupped her hand around his balls and stroked them as she began to suck him. He tasted salty and he felt exquisitely hard and Lexi felt the hot rush of excitement flooding through her veins. She could never be the wife he needed but she could still make this powerful man groan helplessly beneath her lips.

She teased him and taunted him; licked him until he muttered something urgently in Greek and she felt the imperceptible change in his body. He tensed. The fingers which were tangled in her hair were now pressing urgently against her head. She heard him draw in a shuddering breath and then hold it as if it were the last breath he might ever take, before he began to convulse helplessly. She heard the low cry he made as that first warm, salty taste of him spurted into her mouth and she sucked on it greedily, as if it were lifeblood.

She waited until he was still and then drew her mouth away, trying to compose herself, but it wasn't easy.

For a moment he said nothing, just rested his hands on top of her still-damp hair as if he was conferring some sort of blessing. Then he pulled her to her feet before bending to yank up his jeans, wincing slightly as he zipped them up.

But his eyes were serious as he tilted her chin with his hand, capturing her gaze so that she could look nowhere but at him.

'You're very good,' he said.

She licked her lips and she could still taste him. 'I was taught by the best.'

His gaze followed the movement of her tongue as predictably as a cat watching a piece of dangling string.

'As an example of how well you've learned, you certainly couldn't have bettered that little demonstration.'

She wanted to say that it hadn't been a *demonstration*—but how else would she describe it? Lust, certainly. But not just lust. Lust alone didn't make your heart pound with a power which made you feel dizzy. Nor did it make you want to touch your lover's face with a tenderness which might just give away how much you really cared. How much you really loved. Still. Even now.

But none of it mattered. Time was running out. After the christening she would be free to go, because that was what Xenon had told her would happen and he never reneged on a deal.

She managed a smile—a bright beam of a thing which went no further than her lips. 'I'm glad you enjoyed it. It'll be something to remember me by when I'm gone. And while we're on the subject—I'd like to get away as soon as possible tomorrow. I'm happy to go back on a commercial flight if that would be less hassle.'

There was a pause. He seemed to be picking out his words with particular care. 'And what if I said I didn't want you to go?'

Lexi wrinkled her nose. 'But we can't stay here.'

'I'm not proposing we do. But we can go back to London, can't we? We can even go to your place in Devon if that's what you want.'

'Together?'

'Why not?'

For a moment, Lexi got a bizarre image of what it

might be like with Xenon trying to blend into village life. She pictured him standing in a queue in the little corner shop while he waited to buy a loaf of bread. Playing darts in the local pub. Confused now, she stared at him. 'I don't know what you're suggesting.'

'I want to make it with you, Lex,' he said simply. 'I want to give our marriage another chance.'

'But we've already talked about it. We've said everything there is to say.' Her words sounded miraculously strong but she could see from the look on his face that he wasn't really listening to them. And maybe this was inevitable. Maybe she needed to expose the one last, weak link which would sever their relationship for ever.

'No,' he said and his face was filled with a dark determination which made Lexi's heart begin to sink. 'We haven't talked about how we might heal the past. I saw your face when you held Ianthe yesterday. I saw the sadness in your eyes and I understood what you were feeling. But it doesn't have to be this way, Lex. We can start again. We can have another baby—'

'No!' The word came out more violently than she had intended. She could see that its vehemence shocked him—it even shocked her. 'I can't have another baby, Xenon. Don't you understand? That's why this marriage could never work then—or now. Because I can't give you the baby you've always wanted.'

CHAPTER ELEVEN

THERE WAS COMPLETE silence as Xenon stared at Lexi with incomprehension in his dark eyes.

'What are you talking about?'

'The baby was…was…' Her voice began to wobble. What words could she possibly use that wouldn't insult the memory of that little scrap? 'They did…tests. They said that he had a genetic abnormality. Something was wrong with his chromosomes and that was why it had happened. That his condition was not…' She sucked in a shuddering breath as the corrosive truth came out in a bitter rush. 'Was not compatible with life.'

There was a long, disbelieving pause while he looked at her as if he'd never really seen her before. 'And why didn't you tell me this at the time?' he demanded. 'Why the hell didn't you *tell* me, Lex? A secret as big as this and yet you *kept it from me*?'

Pain ripped through her. And guilt. So *much* guilt. 'Because you *weren't there to tell*!' She shook her head. 'Oh, I'm not blaming you for the fact that a volcanic ash cloud brought the global aviation system grinding to a halt—even you couldn't overcome that. But I was having difficulty getting my own head around what the doctors had told me and when you got back you were so…*distant.*'

'Because I didn't know what to say,' he gritted out.

'I know that!' Her voice was wobbling now. Didn't he see? Didn't he understand that there was a reason she had spared him the bitter truth? 'But I also knew you wanted another baby. And that's the bottom line. Because *I can't give you that baby, Xenon.*'

He was staring at her warily, as if he wasn't quite sure what she might do next. 'I still don't understand where you're going with this,' he said.

'Don't you? It's really very simple.' She took a deep breath, which seemed to scorch its way right down into the base of her lungs. 'The reason our baby died was *my fault*, okay? It was *my fault.* Do you understand now?'

He shook his head. 'You can't know that!'

'Yes! Yes, I can!' Lexi dug her nails into her palms, wishing that she could just close her lips and refuse to say any more because it was so painful. But she knew she could not let this go until he accepted the truth. Because she owed him that. He needed to understand that there was no magic wand to be waved to give him what he had always wanted. 'The doctors told me that you can change a lot of things—but you can't change your genetic make-up. And there's something in me which makes it impossible to carry a baby to term. Don't you hear what I'm saying, Xenon? That I'm damaged goods and I'll never be able to guarantee you the son and heir you've always longed for.'

'You're not damaged,' he ground out. 'You're whole and you're beautiful—inside and out!'

He moved to hold her but she held up her hand to stop him. 'No. I'm not. I wish I was, but I'm not.' She backed away from him, wanting to put physical distance between them. Terrified that if she didn't she would weaken and she loved him too much to short-change him for the rest of his life. 'This is your let-out clause, Xenon, don't you see? Don't let some misplaced sense of loyalty or pride make you feel you've got to make it work with me. Don't allow my physical shortcomings to crush your dreams. Go away and find another woman— the right kind of woman—and have a baby with her.'

His breathing was rapid and his eyes were glittering with a hectic blue fire but the words he bit out were strong and steady. 'And what if I told you that I want you, anyway? That, contrary to what your ridiculously low self-esteem might tell you, I did not marry you because you were a "brood mare"? I married you because I loved you. I still do.'

'Don't.' The word came out in a low moan of pain. 'Please don't make this even harder.'

'I'll make it as hard as it damned well needs to be. I'll do whatever I have to do to make you see sense.'

'I *am* being sensible,' she said stubbornly.

'No, you're not. Listen to me, Lex. Yes, I wanted a baby with you—I can't deny that. But maybe there's still a chance we can. We can get a second opinion. We can have access to the best doctors in the world—'

'No.' And maybe the certainty in her voice made

him realise that she was serious because suddenly he tensed. She hugged her arms around her bikini-clad body but beneath it she was still shivering. 'Don't you realise that this is something your money can't buy, or fix? I can't have your baby, Xenon—that's the beginning and the end of it—and because of that, we have no future together.'

His body was tense now; his face dark and brooding. 'So I don't get any say in this?'

She shook her head. 'No.'

'Do you love me?'

Lexi hesitated. Say no, she urged herself. Tell him that all your love has gone—worn out and washed away. But as she looked into his blue eyes she knew she couldn't lie. Her body might have failed him, but her heart would always be true. 'I'll always love you,' she said. 'And it's because of that that I'm setting you free.'

'How very magnanimous of you,' he said. 'You castigate me for being a control freak and now you're telling me it's over without considering any other option.'

'Because there is no other option!'

'Oh, but there is. It's just one that neither of us has considered until now.'

'And that is?'

'That is that we don't go down the baby route. We'll forget about a family—'

'Xenon—'

'Plenty of couples have decent and fulfilled lives without children. If you want—*if you want*—we can think about adoption some time in the future. Or we can just enjoy our niece and the children my cousins will one day have. The children that your own brothers might have. Because I love you, too, Lex—and that love is unconditional. I want you—just you—and whatever comes with having you is all right by me.'

His words were soft with conviction and Lex's heart sang with hope as for a moment she allowed herself to dream for one unbearably beautiful moment. Only this wasn't a dream. It was real. Xenon loved her and she could have his love. She could live with him for the rest of her life. Lexi and Xenon.

But the shadow of reality darkened her thoughts, because how long before their love was spoiled by the nagging recognition of what they were missing? Wouldn't the day come when Xenon would look around and realise he wanted a child, no matter what he said now? Mightn't he decide that he'd made the wrong decision and find himself a fertile woman who could give him his heart's desire? She doubted that people would blame him if he did that.

Her voice was tight—mainly because her heart was beating so fast that she could barely speak. 'My mind is made up,' she said. 'And you aren't going to be able to change it. I can't do it, Xenon. You can't see it now, but one day you're going to thank me for this.'

'*Thank* you?' he echoed, his voice harsh and bitter as his cobalt gaze sliced through her.

She fought to keep her thoughts in order, to push away her own pain and to convince him that this was the only way. 'Yes. Because you love family,' she said simply. 'Even your one foray into the world of film-making involved fatherhood. You once told me that your biggest desire was to become a father yourself, and I can't take that desire away from you, Xenon. I just can't do it.'

He was trembling as he caught hold of her. His hands gripped her arms and Lexi could feel herself trembling, too. His eyes were blazing blue fire and his skin seemed to stretch tightly over his tense face. For one split second she thought he might be about to kiss her. And if he did—if he *did*—then wouldn't she inevitably come round to his way of thinking? Wouldn't she weaken enough to let him convince her that their love was enough to sustain them, and they could forgo the family he had always yearned for?

But he didn't kiss her. The look he subjected her to must have lasted only a total of ten seconds but afterwards she was left feeling as if a cold wind had whipped through her.

He let her go and she stumbled off to the bathroom, loudly locking the door behind her to make sure he heard. Terrified that he would come in and realise that her resolve was far less determined than her words would have him believe.

She still had the christening to get through. She still had to put on the lovely dress she'd packed specially, and do her hair, and make like it mattered. And even though nothing seemed to matter other than that the final curtain had come down on her marriage, Lexi knew that this day was important to Kyra and her family.

But she was sick with nerves as she emerged from

the bathroom to find Xenon already dressed in a light linen suit, his face dark and unwelcoming. She wanted to say something—anything—which would make him understand that this was all for the best. She even tried to smile. 'Xenon—'

'Not now, Lexi,' he iced out. 'I've had about as much from you as I can tolerate this morning.'

And he slammed out of the villa.

She felt like a fraud as she slipped the dress on over her head, practising a happy smile in the mirror even though inside her heart felt as if it were breaking. Just before eleven, she walked outside, where the car was waiting to take them to the small church in Lindos where the ceremony was to be held.

Marina was just about to get in and she nodded approvingly as she assessed Lexi's outfit.

'You look very beautiful, my dear. Xenon has already gone down to the church and he is waiting for us there.'

He's not waiting for me, thought Lexi grimly as the car pulled away, with the bright Greek sunlight bouncing off its polished livery.

The chapel was very old and so tiny that there was room for only twenty people, with the rest standing outside clustered beneath a canopy of olive trees which provided welcome shade.

Lexi was taken aback by the size of the crowd there. Not only was there a giant contingent of the extended Kanellis clan, but plenty of locals and tourists had also turned out to watch. There were cousins, uncles and aunts who seemed disproportionately pleased to see her again—but the only things Lexi could focus on were the forbidding features and piercing blue eyes of her husband.

She had to swallow the stupid sob which was rearing up in her throat, like one of those jungle snakes you sometimes saw on television documentaries.

Xenon stepped forward to usher her inside and she shot him an anxious look. 'I'll wait outside. Your mother says the church is only tiny.'

'You will not. You will be by my side, supporting me as we agreed,' he said. 'And after that you can run back to your empty little life in England.'

The tiny church was cool and at any other time Lexi would have been blown away by its simple beauty and by the moving ceremony which followed. As it was, her emotions were in such turmoil that she could scarcely breathe. She kept thinking of the man beside her. She kept thinking about how hard it was going to be to leave. Last time she'd walked away she had done it because she'd felt as if she'd had no option—that she could not ruin the life of a man who so badly wanted a family of his own.

But this time, he had offered her an option—and she knew she couldn't take it. No matter what he said now, she knew that he would go mad if their lives were to become one constant round of doctors' appointments. And she would go mad if she had to live with the fear that one day he would feel deprived without a blood family of his own.

No. She was doing this for the best. She was doing

this because she loved him and one day he would re-alise that.

There was much cheering and clapping as baby Ianthe began to squall with fury when water was poured over her head—and soon afterwards the convoy of cars began to make its way back up towards the Kanellis estate.

At the party which followed, Lexi stuck to water rather than the champagne with which everyone was toasting the baby. She hung back and waited until there was a lull in all the celebrations before she went over to Kyra and gave her the small package she'd brought with her from England.

'What is this?' Kyra began to unwrap it, folds of tissue paper falling away as she pulled out a delicate silver charm. 'Oh, Lexi—it's a unicorn! Did you make it?'

'I did.' Lexi smiled. 'A mythical beast which was discovered by a Greek historian.'

'Of course. Who else?' laughed Kyra.

'It means power and healing and renewal, among other things. I thought perhaps she could wear it on a chain when she's older.' Lexi looked up to find Xenon standing there and in that moment she thought that her heart might break in two.

'It's beautiful,' he said, his blue eyes piercing into hers.

You're beautiful, she thought. *You're beautiful and I love you but I can't give you want you want.* She stood up, taking in a deep breath as she drew him aside to speak in a low voice. 'Xenon, I can't stay any longer.

It isn't fair to any of us. I want to leave today—to slip away without too much comment.'

His mouth twisted. 'You don't imagine that your absence won't be remarked upon? That you can just fly out of here without anybody noticing you've gone?'

She met his gaze without flinching. 'I'm sure you can sweet-talk your way out of it. You've done it often enough in the past.'

His mouth hardened into a grim replica of a smile. *Not this time,* he thought. *Not this time.*

But while he might want her, he would not dream of stopping her. For what would be the point of keeping a woman who did not want to stay?

CHAPTER TWELVE

LEXI THOUGHT SHE'D welcome being back in her little Devonshire village. That she'd be relieved that her emotions were no longer spiking up and down, like one of those graphs you saw at the bottom of a hospital bed. Somehow she had imagined that life would resume a comfortable pace now that Xenon was no longer in it.

But she had been wrong.

She felt as if a giant light had been snuffed out, leaving her stumbling around in bewildering darkness. The daily routine she'd once loved now seemed empty; her days simply hours she needed to get through before she could escape to bed for yet another sleepless night. Even her jewellery making—something which had given her so much pleasure—now seemed to lack imagination and flair.

She found herself looking blankly at the crude pieces of silver and wondering what on earth to do with them. Where before she would have been bursting with ideas, her imagination seemed to have deserted her.

And she missed Xenon. She'd anticipated that; she just hadn't realised how much. He had taken her back into his world and given her a glimpse of what life with him could be like and she had wanted that life back. God, she had wanted it. But she couldn't have it.

She couldn't have him.

She had left Rhodes with a heavy heart, having first crept into the sick room to kiss his sleeping grandmother goodbye. She'd said farewell to a frankly bewildered Marina, whose innate code of manners clearly prevented her from asking her why she was going so suddenly.

Xenon had kissed her lightly on each cheek just before he'd closed the door on the car taking her to the airport. And in a way, that had been almost worse than if he'd gone into a massive sulk and refused to say goodbye. But no, he had managed to don the suave cloak of civility. He had even managed to slant her a half-smile, though he hadn't quite been able to disguise the furious glitter in his eyes. And Lexi realised that her last memory of the man she loved would be of him giving her the kind of cool kiss he might have offered some casual acquaintance he'd just met at a party.

The last thing she'd asked was for him to give her Jason's contact details and, to her surprise, he had done this without hesitation. He'd explained that the vineyard was extremely remote and that her brother was taking a break from all electronic forms of communication, but that she could write to him there.

And Lexi had. She'd written several times. Long letters, which she'd tried to make cheerful—which hadn't been easy, except for the bits when she told him how proud she was that he was turning his life around. That bit had burst straight from her heart.

The only things she received in return were a couple of postcards—battered old things which looked as if they had been taken when photography was still in its infancy. The messages they contained had been succinct but encouraging.

It's GREAT!

And,

Best time of my LIFE!

Lexi found that she was longing to see him again and she told him so in her next letter, hoping that her motives weren't selfish. That she wasn't just wanting contact with him because her heart felt so empty.

One gloomy November evening, she had just poured herself a cup of tea when she heard the sound of footsteps on gravel, only this time she was paying attention and they were very definitely not the distinctive tread of her estranged husband.

She pulled open the door and for a moment she didn't recognise the man who stood on the doorstep, a rucksack on his back, wearing a jacket which was way too thin for the inclement weather. His hair was bleached blonde, his skin deeply tanned—and he was fit and muscular. He looked like someone she used to know, but only vague physical traces of that person still existed.

'Jason?' Lexi blinked. 'Jason, is that really you?'

'Better get yourself a new pair of glasses, sis. Of course it's me!' Laughing, he dropped his rucksack and gathered her in a fierce hug.

'You'd better come in.'

'Just you try stopping me.' And then he frowned. 'Lexi, you're looking awfully *thin*.'

'Rubbish.' She shut the door and smiled at him. 'Have you eaten?'

'Not since lunchtime.'

Over mushroom risotto he told her everything that had happened. How much he loved working outside, on the land. 'But it's more than that, Lexi,' he said, tearing off a huge hunk of garlic bread. 'Wine-making is so complex—and Greek wine has the potential to really do something spectacular in the marketplace—the way Australian wine did decades ago. And Xenon is pleased with what I've been doing. In fact, he's offered to give me a permanent role in the family vineyards if I want it. And I do.'

Ah yes, Xenon. The one name she hadn't mentioned. The massive elephant in the room as far as Lexi was concerned, although Jason clearly had no such reservations. He said his brother-in-law's name with a mixture of loyalty, affection and the faintest trace of hero worship.

'It was very decent of him to help you,' she ventured.

'Yes, it was.' Jason's silvery-green eyes—so like her own, only without the myopic tendencies—started shining with enthusiasm. 'Without being too melodramatic about it, I owe him my life. If he hadn't come and found me and plucked me out of the gutter, I don't know where I'd be today.'

There was complete silence. With a hand which

wasn't quite steady, Lexi put her fork down on her plate. 'What are you talking about? You went to *him*, didn't you? You asked *him* for money because you were in terrible debt.'

'Is that what he told you?' Jason grinned and swopped his empty plate with her still almost full one. 'The debt bit was right—but I didn't ask Xenon for help. I think I was past the stage of knowing I needed it, when he suddenly appeared out of nowhere and told me he was going to give me one last chance to turn my life around. But that if I blew it, there wouldn't be another.'

He finished off Lexi's risotto. Then started talking about integrating into Greek village life and a young woman he'd met who now made such integration seem vital, but Lexi barely took in a word he was saying.

She didn't understand.

Xenon had come to her and made it sound as if Jason was demanding financial help—and that he would withhold that help without her co-operation. But now Jason was telling her that *Xenon* had been the instigator. That he had gone to her brother and offered him a solution to his problem.

Why had he done that?

There was only one reason she could think of. The same reason he'd given her for wanting to stay married to her—childless or not. Because he loved her. Because he'd never stopped loving her.

Oh, God.

She made herself coffee and poured Jason a second

glass of wine. 'Do you happen to know where Xenon is?' she asked casually.

'Sure. He's in Hollywood. It's the tenth anniversary of *My Crazy Greek Father* coming up and there are loads of celebrations planned.'

Lexi chewed on her thumbnail. Athens would have been simpler and London simpler still. Hollywood seemed like a scary kind of place and one she'd moved on from a long time ago. And could she really risk making a transatlantic flight on the evidence of a single fact which might no longer mean anything?

She felt the twist of pain in her heart.

Could she risk *not* doing it?

With Jason sleeping soundly in the spare room, she tossed and turned all night, trying to reinforce all the reasons why it was best to leave things as they were. But the morning brought with it nothing but a burning certainty that she couldn't let matters rest.

'How long are you staying?' she asked Jason.

He shrugged. 'That depends how long you'll have me. I'm not due back in Athens for a couple of weeks.'

She tossed him a spare set of keys. 'Stay as long as you like. I have to go away for a few days.'

She could see the look of gratitude on his face and she guessed her offer was yet another mark of his successful rehabilitation. She would never have allowed him the freedom of her house before now.

She hadn't booked a flight in a long time—actually, when she stopped to think about it, she'd *never* booked a flight for herself. Her management had always done it when she was in The Lollipops and when she'd been with Xenon, his private jet had always been at her disposal.

It was a fiddly business but she sorted out her ticket and all the entry requirements she needed to get into the US, and three days later her plane passed the giant Lego-like skyscrapers of Los Angeles, before coming in to land.

The palms of her hands were clammy and her stomach was tying itself up in knots. She hadn't told Jason she was coming here and she certainly hadn't warned Xenon of her plans. She wanted to see the expression on his face when he saw her again. She was scared that his love for her might have died. She was scared that he might now have considered himself lucky to have escaped from the prospect of a childless marriage.

She knew he always stayed at the hotel on Wilshire Boulevard owned by his friend Zak Constantinides, but, of course, all that could have changed. These days he might have changed his allegiance to one of the newer, trendier places on Sunset Boulevard, which she'd discovered on the Internet. Nevertheless, she'd booked into Zak's hotel, even if the room rates had made her eyes water.

She waited until she had taken her bags upstairs before she dialled Xenon's number and her heart started pounding when he picked it up on the third ring.

'Lex,' he said, his voice sardonic and not particularly welcoming. 'This *is* a surprise.'

'Yes, I realise that. I want to… I wondered if we could have a talk.'

'I got the distinct impression we'd said everything there was to say.'

There was no softening in his voice. Not a single hint that he was pleased to hear from her. She sensed that he wasn't going to make this easy for her. She was going to have to face the fact that it might be too late. *Please, God, let it not be too late.* 'Could we?' she persisted.

'Go ahead. Talk. I'm not stopping you.'

'I meant face to face.'

'You might have a little difficulty with that one. I'm in Hollywood.'

'So am I.'

A brief silence followed.

'What did you say?'

'I'm in Hollywood. Actually, I'm in Zak's hotel and I'm wondering if you are, too. Jason told me you were over here, so I made a stab at guessing where you'd be staying.'

'Presidential suite,' he snapped and cut the connection.

Lexi told herself she should have waited before calling him. She should at least have given herself time to wash the long flight out of her system. As it was, there was barely time to splash cold water on her face and brush her hair into some kind of order before she took the lift up to the penthouse suite.

The door was on the latch and she pushed it open.

'Xenon?'

'I'm in here.'

She followed the direction of the voice, her heart clenching at the sound of his forbidding tone. She told herself it was probably too late. Of course it was too late.

He was standing in the sumptuous main reception area—all glowing shades of gold and claret. Tulips the colour of burgundy added to the almost medieval feel of the room and, in complete contrast, Xenon added a note of dark formality. He was wearing a black tuxedo and the exquisite suit made Lexi feel like the hired help in her jeans and T-shirt.

But his blue eyes were cold and he made a rather ostentatious show of glancing at his wristwatch. 'You have half an hour before I'm due at a reception downtown,' he said. 'So you'd better get a move on.'

Suddenly she didn't know where to begin. She wondered if she'd pushed him too far.

'Jason came to see me.'

'I thought he might once the harvest was over.'

She sucked in her lips. 'He told me what happened.'

'Anything in particular?' he enquired unhelpfully. 'How good the grape yield was? How he seems to have fallen for one of the local women?'

'He told me that he didn't come to you, asking for your help,' she whispered. 'That you went and found him out and offered it and I was wondering…' She cleared her throat. 'I was wondering just why you did that.'

But if she was hoping for a softening of his obdurate features, she was in for a disappointment because the only reaction she got was the contemptuous curve of his lips.

'I think we both know exactly why I did it, Lexi. I wanted a legitimate way back into your life. I wanted to give our relationship one last go. Which I did. And I found out what I needed to know. It's over. We're over—we both know that. So why are you here?'

She wanted to curl up and die because the expression in his eyes was so *cold*. She'd never seen him look like that before and she felt the chill whisper of foreboding.

'Because...' She sucked in a deep breath. 'Because finding that out...discovering that it wasn't just some random act that brought you back into my life, well, that made a difference. It made me realise how important our marriage was to you. It made me examine what I was doing. It made me realise what I was about to throw away.'

He shook his dark head, tugging at his black bow tie as if he was impatient to be away. 'You're just focusing on a detail,' he said. 'Not on what is important. And what's important is that you don't want to make a life with me on any terms—you told me that yourself. But it's okay. I'll survive, Lex. We'll both survive.'

'But I don't know if I will.' Her voice sounded as light as a feather. 'Because surviving doesn't sound like a good way to live. Not when I consider the alternative. I meant it when I said that I love you, Xenon—I've never really stopped, even though I've tried hard enough. If you want the truth—my life has been...well, awful without you. And if you're prepared—I mean, really prepared—to accept a marriage without children, then you only have to say the word. Just say the word, my darling, and I'll be back in your arms so quick you won't even have time to blink.'

His mouth tightened as he looked at her and she was aware of the ice which had hardened his cobalt eyes. 'Get out,' he said and turned his back on her as if he found the view outside the window infinitely more alluring.

Lexi stared in disbelief at the forbidding set of his shoulders, at the coiled tension in his tuxedoed body, which was contrasted against the busy rush of Wilshire Boulevard.

'You don't mean that,' she whispered, her heart pounding with fear.

'Oh, but I do,' he said grimly. 'You think I'm your puppet, do you, Lex? That if you keep me dangling long enough I'll dance exactly to your tune? Well, you had your chance and you blew it. Sorry.'

Lexi felt the tears begin to well up in her eyes. Hot, salty tears which mocked her and told her that she'd left it too late. Xenon didn't want her any more and it really *was* over. For a split second she thought about turning and fleeing from the room and this terrible pain which was tearing at her heart. But she was through with running away and, besides, something about the way he spoke jarred. And not just in the way he spoke, but in the way he was holding himself, with his fists clenched and his shoulders now hunched. He looked like a man

And then he started to kiss her. He kissed her until she was dizzy with longing and when he let her go she was so happy that she wanted to dance around the fancy suite. But then she noticed that he was glancing at his watch and that he was frowning.

'You know, I really do have to be downtown very soon,' he said. 'If it was any other engagement, I'd break it—but this film means a lot of things to a lot of people and I want to put a very positive image of Greece out there. But if you want me to stay—'

'Go,' she said, lifting her hand to his cheek and stroking it. 'I can wait here until you get back.'

'Well, you can. Or you could ride across town with me to where a great deal of the world's press will be assembled, and we could give them a picture which will tell the world that we are very definitely back together. Because I have this insane and very uncharacteristic desire to want to shout it from the rooftops.'

Lexi looked down at her crumpled jeans and T-shirt, before lifting her gaze to the pristine appearance of his tuxedo. 'You mean, like this?' she questioned doubtfully.

He smiled. 'I mean exactly like that.'

'When every other woman there will be dripping in sequins and diamonds?'

'Who cares? There's no woman to compare with you—no matter what you wear.'

'Oh, Xenon. You do say the most gorgeous things.'

'Well, that's only because you *are* the most gorgeous

thing.' He lifted her hand to his lips and kissed it. 'So come along, Mrs Kanellis. Because the sooner I take you out, the sooner I can get you home.'

EPILOGUE

THE SUNLIGHT FELT warm on his eyelids and her thigh felt cool against his. Lazily, Xenon stretched his arms above his head and yawned.

'So you're awake at last.'

Lexi's soft words filtered through the air towards him, like the breeze which floated in from the park outside. The uncharacteristically hot, English summer they'd been having meant that most nights they slept with the windows wide open. Sometimes Xenon even woke up imagining he was back in Greece!

He opened his eyes to find Lexi leaning over him and her long hair tickled his chest as she reached over to retrieve her glasses.

'Actually, I've been awake for a while,' he murmured, sliding his hand around her waist and pulling her close, so that he could breathe in her particular scent of violets and vanilla. 'Enjoying this rare lie-in and just counting up all my blessings.'

'Oh?' Lexi snuggled closer. 'And what blessings might they be?'

'You know perfectly well what they are,' he teased.

'Because you're my perfect wife who gives me a perfect life.'

She touched her fingertips to his jaw and began to stroke reflectively at the dark, new growth there. 'I'm not perfect, Xenon.'

'Yes, you are. Perfect for me.'

Lexi hugged him very tightly as she kissed his bare chest, brushing her lips over the whorls of dark hair there and letting her tongue trace tiny patterns over the hard, salty flesh. Sometimes this all felt so good that she almost had to pinch herself to believe it was happening. But it was. And Xenon had been right all along. Two people who loved one another could live a contented and fulfilled life with or without children. Her inability to carry a child had not damaged their relationship. On the contrary, the heartache they had suffered had ended up bringing them closer together.

And then something had happened which had changed their lives completely, in a way they could never have foreseen. Lexi had been watching a TV programme about the shortage of foster parents and had been deeply affected by the plight of some of the children featured. It hadn't taken much for her to persuade Xenon to donate a significant amount of money to The Children's Society, nor for her to become involved on a volunteer basis. But neither of them expected to be so enchanted by a nine-month-old baby who'd been orphaned in a car crash, nor for their offer of a temporary home to be transformed into the opportunity to adopt her permanently.

There was, as Xenon said afterwards, really no decision to make, for by that time they had fallen hopelessly in love with the little girl and she with them. They named her Sofia after his beloved grandmother.

Now almost four, Sofia was almost exactly the same age as their niece, Ianthe, and the reason for the rare lie-in was because Xenon's sister had brought her family over for a week's holiday. Kyra and Nikola had taken Sofia and her cousin for a walk in Regent's Park and afterwards they were having a trip to the famous zoo.

'Which leaves me all morning to make slow and delicious love to you,' Xenon murmured.

He drifted his mouth over her breast and she bit her lip in delighted response. Skin touched skin. Gasps punctured the air. Lexi lifted her hips to meet him, a shaft of intense pleasure coursing through her as he filled her completely.

Afterwards she kissed him, long and lazy kisses. 'What did I ever do to deserve you?' she said, her words muffled by the pressure of his lips.

'That's my question.' His voice was sleepy. 'And you already know the answer. Don't analyse. Just be grateful.'

And she was. Oh, she was.

Despite the joys and commitment of motherhood, she had continued to make her quirky jewellery on a part-time basis and soon it began to feature in magazines. Before long she was having to take on two workers to help craft Gibson Gems. Anyone who was anyone had a pair of her dangly earrings, or one of her distinctively chunky bangles. Her client base included three members of the English royal family, as well as most of Hollywood. But Lexi never forgot the people of Devon who'd been so kind to her when she'd been starting out, and every year she travelled down to sell her jewellery at the village's Christmas fayre.

Jason married his Greek girlfriend and Xenon went on to appoint him CEO of the Kanellis wine industry. Within the year, Lexi's other brother, Jake, flew from Australia to join the company, which meant that Lexi could see much more of them. Both brothers became fluent in Greek and, after much nagging, persuaded Lexi to take lessons. She didn't find it easy but she was determined—and she loved the look of shock on her husband's face the first time she answered him fluently in his mother tongue.

After much persuasion on Xenon's part—because he seemed to be determined to make a statement to the world—Lexi agreed to a renewal of their wedding vows, in a ceremony which took place in the beautiful Greek cathedral in Bayswater, London. Afterwards they held a huge party held in the ballroom at the Granchester Hotel. Security was tight and the place was mobbed because Roxy and Justina—the other two Lollipops— were on the guest list. It was unexpectedly moving to see her ex-bandmates again and there had been quite a few tears when all three women had taken part in a group hug while 'Come Right Back' played over the sound system.

Xenon had bought her a new wedding ring for the

occasion, though—as Lexi had pointed out—she was probably the only woman in the world who owned three wedding rings, all given to her by the same man.

'Ah, but this time it's different, *moli mou*,' he had murmured. 'This time it's for ever.'

Their favourite photo was not of that day, nor indeed any of those taken on their original wedding day. It was an image captured the night when Lexi had flown to Hollywood to tell Xenon how much she loved him and he'd taken her downtown, to a fancy reception to mark his Oscar-winning film.

There was Xenon, tall and magnificent in an immaculate tuxedo, with Lexi beside him in jeans and a T-shirt still crumpled from her long, transatlantic flight.

But you didn't really notice the discrepancy in what they were wearing, or the fact that Lexi's hair looked as if it could have done with a good brushing. All you saw was the light which shone from their eyes, which even the most cynical observers had remarked was brighter than all the flashes from the assembled cameras.

That light was love.

* * * * *

A sneaky peek at next month…

MODERN™

INTERNATIONAL AFFAIRS, SEDUCTION & PASSION GUARANTEED

My wish list for next month's titles…

In stores from 18th October 2013:

❑ Million Dollar Christmas Proposal – Lucy Monroe

❑ The Consequences of That Night – Jennie Lucas

❑ Visconti's Forgotten Heir – Elizabeth Power

❑ A Touch of Temptation – Tara Pammi

In stores from 1st November 2013:

❑ A Dangerous Solace – Lucy Ellis

❑ Secrets of a Powerful Man – Chantelle Shaw

❑ Never Gamble with a Caffarelli – Melanie Milburne

❑ The Rogue's Fortune – Cat Schield

Available at WHSmith, Tesco, Asda, Eason, Amazon and Apple

Just can't wait?

1013/01

Special Offers

Every month we put together collections and longer reads written by your favourite authors.

Here are some of next month's highlights— and don't miss our fabulous discount online!

On sale 1st November   On sale 1st November   On sale 18th October

Find out more at
www.millsandboon.co.uk/specialreleases

Visit us Online

1113/ST/MB440

Come home this Christmas to Fiona Harper

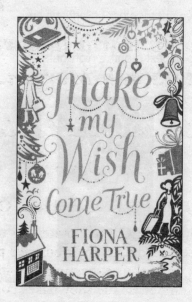

From the author of *Kiss Me Under the Mistletoe* comes a Christmas tale of family and fun. Two sisters are ready to swap their Christmases—the busy super-mum, Juliet, getting the chance to escape it all on an exotic Christmas getaway, whilst her glamorous work-obsessed sister, Gemma, is plunged headfirst into the family Christmas she always thought she'd hate.

www.millsandboon.co.uk

Wrap up warm this winter with Sarah Morgan…

Sleigh Bells in the Snow

Kayla Green loves business and hates Christmas.

So when Jackson O'Neil invites her to Snow Crystal Resort to discuss their business proposal… the last thing she's expecting is to stay for Christmas dinner. As the snowflakes continue to fall, will the woman who doesn't believe in the magic of Christmas finally fall under its spell…?

4th October

www.millsandboon.co.uk/sarahmorgan

1013/MB435

JOSIE SMITH IN SUMMER

Magdalen Nabb

Illustrated by Karen Donnelly

Galaxy

CHIVERS PRESS
BATH

First published 2000
by
Collins
This Large Print edition published by
Chivers Press
by arrangement with
HarperCollins Publishers
2001

ISBN 0 7540 6164 7

British Library Cataloguing in Publication Data

Nabb, Magdalen, 1947–
 Josie Smith in summer.—Large print ed.
 1. Smith, Josie (Fictitious character)
 2.Children's stories 3. Large type books
 I. Title
 823. 9'14[J]

ISBN 0-7540-6164-7

Printed and bound in Great Britain by
BOOKCRAFT, Midsomer Norton, Somerset

CONTENTS

JOSIE SMITH AND FRIENDS

Josie Smith

Ginger

Mum

Eileen

Gran

Geoffrey Taylor

Gary Grimes

Jimmy Earnshaw

Rawley Baxter

Rawley's sister

Miss Potts

Mr Scowcroft

Mr Kefford

Mrs Chadwick

Ann Lomax

Tahara

Josie Smith Goes Fishing

On the first day of the summer holidays, Josie Smith got up early and washed her hands and face. She put on a flowered summer frock that her mum had made her last year. She wanted to look nice because she was going out with Geoffrey Taylor and Geoffrey Taylor's dad. Then she went downstairs to the kitchen door and put her wellingtons on because they were going fishing. She had butterflies in her tummy because she'd never been fishing before. She went out in the yard. The sun was hot and fresh and her mum was hanging up some washing that smelled cool and soapy.

'Mum?' said Josie Smith. 'Can I have my breakfast because I've got to hurry up.'

'What have you got to hurry up for?' asked Josie's mum. She said it in a funny voice because she had a clothes peg in her mouth.

Josie Smith was worried. Had her mum forgotten she was going fishing with Geoffrey Taylor? Would there be no sandwiches for her to take? How could grown-ups forget really important things when they always remembered about washing behind

3

your ears?

'I'm going fishing,' said Josie Smith, 'with Geoffrey Taylor and Geoffrey Taylor's dad and I have to take sandwiches.'

Josie's mum pegged up a white pillow case and then unpegged it again. 'Look at the stain on this,' she said. 'Have you been colouring in bed again?'

'I might have been...' said Josie Smith with her eyes half shut. She always shut her eyes if it was a lie but she couldn't remember whether she'd been colouring in bed or not.

'I'll have to try a bit of bleach on it,' said Josie's mum to herself, and she went inside with the pillow case, saying, 'How many times have I told you about colouring in bed? There are more books and toys than there are bedclothes on that bed. And I hope you made your bed before you came down. Well?'

'I was just going to,' said Josie Smith and she dashed back upstairs. She was really worried about being late now. Would Geoffrey Taylor and Geoffrey

4

Taylor's dad set off without her?

In her bedroom she got hold of Percy Panda and loved him. 'You have to get up, Percy, because I've got to make the bed. You can sit on the windowsill where you can see down into the yard. Look, there's Ginger sitting on the roof of the shed.'

So Percy sat on the windowsill looking out and Josie Smith started making her bed. When she tidied the books under her pillow she did find a colouring book, so perhaps she had been colouring in bed a bit. The green was missing from her colours and she had to dive right down to the bottom under the bedclothes to look for it. She felt around for a long time until she heard 'click'. It had fallen down under the bed.

Josie Smith got off the bed and crawled underneath to find it. The green looked a bit fluffy but she blew on it and put it in a tidy line with the others on her colouring book. Then she tidied up the book she was reading and the book she was going to read next and her favourite book of ballet

5

that she read all the time and put her pillow back nice and straight on top of everything. Then she put Percy back to bed and kissed his fat woolly face and tucked him in. She had made her bed.

Downstairs, Josie's mum had put the pillow case to soak and she was getting their breakfast ready.

'Mum, I'm going fishing today with Geoffrey Taylor and Geoffrey Taylor's dad,' said Josie Smith.

'Not without your breakfast you're not,' said Josie's mum. 'Sit down.'

'I am sitting down,' said Josie Smith, 'and, Mum, I've got to take sandwiches. Mum, don't you remember?'

'No,' said Josie's mum, 'I'd forgotten. Have you washed behind those ears?'

'Yes,' said Josie Smith with her eyes shut.

'Well, eat your breakfast, then,' said Josie's mum.

Josie Smith ate her breakfast but it wasn't so easy because there was a lump in her throat. She thought she wouldn't be ready in time. She thought they might set off without her. She looked at the clock on the mantelpiece and it said a-quarter-to-nine. They were supposed to set off at half-past-ten but Josie Smith didn't know how long it would take to wipe her wellingtons with a damp cloth so they'd be nice and black, and comb her hair and put a ribbon in it—and the sandwiches! If her mum had forgotten, there might be no sandwiches and then what would she do? Would they still let her go with them? Would Geoffrey Taylor give her a sandwich if she didn't have any of her own?

Josie Smith, worrying hard, looked across at her mum.

Her mum was looking out the window at the line of white washing in the yard.

'It'd dry better if there were a bit of a wind,' she said. 'I'll not wash the blankets today.'

'Mum,' said Josie Smith in a tiny, lumpy voice, 'have you really forgotten I'm going fishing?' She wasn't crying but she wasn't breathing either.

Josie's mum reached over and wiggled Josie Smith's nose.

'The day before yesterday,' she said, 'you told me you were going fishing today with Geoffrey Taylor and Geoffrey Taylor's dad.'

'And you haven't forgotten!' said Josie Smith.

'And I haven't forgotten,' said Josie's mum. 'I don't know why it is but I haven't forgotten. Perhaps it's because after you'd told me about it the day before yesterday, you told me again a hundred times. And then yesterday you told me again a hundred and one times. And today, you've already told me three times and you've only been up half an hour. And I might have forgotten for a minute just before you got up if you hadn't left your fishing net and jam-jar parked at the kitchen door where I'd trip over them when I tried to get out with the washing. You'd

8

better tell me again where it is you're going, though. What was it, now . . . did you say you were going for a walk with Gary Grimes?'

'No!' shouted Josie Smith. 'With Geoffrey Taylor and Geoffrey Taylor's dad and we're not going for a walk, we're going fishing! Why are you laughing at me?' Then Josie Smith started laughing, too. Then she looked worried again and said, 'Mum, it's ten-to-nine!'

'You've plenty of time,' said Josie's mum. 'Now, let's have a look at you.'

Josie's mum looked behind Josie Smith's ears and told her to go and wash them and clean her teeth. Then she brushed Josie Smith's hair and said, 'Do you want a ribbon in it?'

'I want a ribbon,' said Josie Smith, 'but I've lost the ribbon for this frock.'

Josie's mum made everybody's frocks and when she made one for Josie Smith she made her a ribbon to match.

'That's your last year's frock,' said Josie's mum, pulling at the skirt, 'or was it the year before? It won't let

9

down any more. Go and look in the big basket. You never know. I've a feeling there's a bit of that stuff left.'

Josie's mum had a huge square basket with a lid where she kept bits of left-over stuff and new pieces that she hadn't used yet. You had to have clean hands to go in it. Josie Smith with clean hands and face and clean teeth— and even almost clean ears—opened the lid and searched for a piece of the red and blue flowered stuff of her frock.

Right at the bottom she found it. 'It's too short,' said Josie Smith.

'It is, isn't it?' said Josie's mum. 'But I know what we can do.'

They went in the front room where the sewing machine was always ready to go because Josie's mum sewed all the time. She sat down now and took a bit of elastic, and in two minutes made

10

Josie Smith an Alice band to match her frock.

Josie Smith polished her wellingtons with a damp cloth.

'Now,' said Josie's mum, 'let's look at you.'

Josie Smith stood still to be looked at. She was a bit worried that her mum might say she had to wear her horrible brown lace-ups because she was going out, but she didn't. She said, 'Are you sure you don't want to wear your shorts for going fishing?'

'No,' said Josie Smith, 'I don't want to look like a boy.'

'You like Geoffrey Taylor, don't you?' said Josie's mum.

'Are you going to marry him instead of Jimmy Earnshaw?'

'No,' said Josie Smith, 'I'm not marrying anybody except Jimmy Earnshaw because he gave me Ginger and because he's big

11

and he's got a two-wheeler and he gives me a ride on it.'

'I see. But you want to look nice to go fishing with Geoffrey Taylor.'

'I don't want to look like a boy. I only like frocks.' She looked at her mum very hard to see if she was going to say she hadn't to get the flowered frock dirty but she didn't. She said, 'Well, it's an old frock so at least it won't matter if it gets ripped and muddy which it will, knowing you, and your wellies will keep your feet dry. Now, go across to Mrs Chadwick's and buy two fresh muffins for your sandwiches.'

Josie Smith went across to Mrs Chadwick's corner shop and said, 'Two muffins, please.'

Mrs Chadwick gave Josie Smith two muffins in a bag and took her money. Then she looked over the counter and down

at Josie Smith.

'You look a comic,' she said, 'in your flowered frock and wellingtons.'

'I'm going fishing,' said Josie Smith, 'that's why.'

'You look a right little comic,' Mrs Chadwick said.

Josie Smith went out, ringing the bell hard on Mrs Chadwick's shop door.

On the doorstep next to Josie Smith's, Eileen was sitting in the sun with her bride doll. Eileen had a flowered frock on with frills and white socks with pink frills round and white shoes.

'You look daft,' said Eileen, 'with your flowered frock and wellingtons.'

'I do not,' said Josie Smith, 'and anyway, I'm going fishing.'

'You still look daft,' Eileen said. 'Everybody'll laugh at you.'

'They will not,' said Josie Smith. 'Just because you can't come . . .'

'I don't want to come,' Eileen said, 'and anyway, I'm going to the hairdresser's on Saturday and I'm having a new frock for the garden fête in the park next week and I'll look nicer than you, so Ner Ner Ner.'

Josie Smith went in and shut the door.

Josie's mum made Josie Smith's favourite sandwiches with fresh muffins and lettuce and sardines and spring onions and egg and tomato and salad cream. She put the muffins back in their paper bag and gave Josie Smith an apple to put in the pocket of her frock.

'Mum, Geoffrey Taylor's dad said I don't have to take a drink because we're going to drink at Judy's spout.'

'I know,' said Josie's mum. 'Get your fishing net and your jam-jar.'

Josie Smith didn't know what Judy's spout was but she didn't want to ask her mum. She just liked the name. She said it over and over to herself as she marched past Eileen with her sandwiches and fishing net, not speaking, and went down the street to Geoffrey Taylor's. 'Judy's spout,' she whispered, 'Judy's spout,' and it sounded like a cold bubbling drink, better than anything you could buy, even at Mrs Chadwick's. When she was nearly at Geoffrey Taylor's house she stopped saying it and she heard Eileen shouting behind her, 'You look stupid and everybody'll laugh at you!'

Josie Smith lifted her fist to knock on Geoffrey Taylor's door, but she didn't knock.

Should she have put her shorts on like her mum said?

Did she look a comic like Mrs Chadwick said?

Did she look stupid like Eileen said?

Would Geoffrey Taylor laugh at her?

Josie Smith looked at the door and

she didn't knock. Then she looked up the street and she didn't see Eileen. Eileen had gone in with her doll. Josie Smith put down her bag of muffins very carefully on Geoffrey Taylor's doorstep and parked her fishing net and jam-jar by the door. That way they would know she was coming. Then she ran back up the street as fast as lightning and crept into her own back yard. Hidden behind the washing she crept to the open kitchen door. Inside she listened and heard the sewing machine going in the front room. She took off her wellingtons and put them back in their place on the mat. Then she crept upstairs in stockinged feet and put on clean, white socks and her white sandals. They were really for best and her mum hadn't let her wear them once since last summer They were hard

16

to put on, perhaps because she wasn't used to them. Then she crept downstairs again and ran off down the street.

Josie Smith liked her best white sandals but she couldn't run in them as fast as she could run in her wellingtons. In fact, she couldn't run fast at all. She couldn't even run. She walked down the street and Geoffrey Taylor and his dad were waiting for her at their door.

'Did you forget something?' asked Geoffrey Taylor's dad.

'Yes,' said Josie Smith with her eyes shut. She couldn't tell them about her sandals. Mr Taylor had wellingtons on but Geoffrey Taylor was wearing old gym shoes and no socks.

'Let's go,' Geoffrey Taylor said. 'Your sandwiches are in my rucksack. Here's your net.'

The three of them set off.

They went down to the main road and then turned off it and went up a steep lane. It was a very long steep lane. Josie Smith was hot.

Geoffrey Taylor's dad told them some very long stories about fishing in lots of different places in the olden days. Josie Smith tried to listen hard but she got the stories a bit muddled up because she was having difficulties. She knew her best sandals weren't so good for running but now they weren't so good for walking, either. Something was hurting her little toe. She thought it might be a lump or crease in her sock. Most times, when her feet hurt it was either a lump or a crease in her sock or else a stone. They hadn't walked on any stones yet. They had walked a long way, though. Josie Smith was hot and sore.

'I remember saying to Tommy

Banks, I said, "I don't think we'll ever get a day's fishing like today's" and we never did.'

'Did you not, Mr Taylor?'

'We didn't,' said Geoffrey Taylor's dad, 'never. You're a slow walker, aren't you?'

'No,' said Josie Smith. 'I'm a fast walker and a fast runner as well.'

'Let's be having you, then,' said Geoffrey Taylor's dad, 'or you'll have it dark.'

Josie Smith didn't want to tell him about the crease or lump because she didn't want him to think she was soft. She walked a bit faster and smiled very hard so nobody would notice there was anything wrong. She was hot and sore and thirsty.

Geoffrey Taylor's dad started another story and Geoffrey Taylor said to Josie Smith, 'My dad's been in the army and he's been to hundreds of places. What's up with your foot?'

'Nothing,' said Josie Smith, smiling harder. 'Why does your dad talk about the olden days? Does he not like it now?'

'No, he doesn't and I don't either because I've got no mum.'

At the top of the lane was a building. It was shaped a bit like a church with a little porch but it was only as big as one room. Over the door it said SCHOOL.

'My grandfather went to this school,' said Geoffrey Taylor's dad, 'and this is Judy's spout.'

Josie Smith looked. Next to the little old school, in a patch of dandelions and buttercups, was a stone face with a spout coming out of the mouth, that bubbled and gurgled fresh cold water into a square stone trough that was green with moss. Josie Smith was hot and sore and very, very thirsty. She knelt down in the tickly buttercups and drank. The water from Judy's

spout was icy cold and bubbly and pure, as clear as the blue sky and as fresh as the buttercups.

Josie Smith drank and drank and let the bubbly water run over her hot face. It really was better than any drink you could buy, even from Mrs Chadwick's. When they had all had a drink, Geoffrey Taylor's dad filled a metal container with a green canvas cover on it so they'd have some to drink with their sandwiches. Then they went on up the road and climbed a stile on the left to go into Tag Wood. First there was a field of buttercups and they picked one to hold under their chins to see who liked butter best and it was Josie Smith. Then, in the shade of the big trees there were bluebells with perfume so strong it took your breath away. Josie Smith liked the bluebells so much she forgot how her foot was hurting. The cool bluebells tickled her legs and the perfume made her smile and then they went down a steep path to the stream that chattered and bubbled over big, mossy stones.

Josie Smith,
hot and sore,
wished she
could take her
shoes and
socks off and
cool her feet in
the stream.

'Come on,' said Mr Taylor, 'take your shoes and socks off. Don't you want to paddle?'

Josie Smith and Geoffrey Taylor sat down and pulled off their shoes and socks and put their hot feet in the bubbling water, squealing because it was so nice and cold. Then Geoffrey Taylor said, 'What's that?' and looked at Josie Smith's foot. 'It's been bleeding,' he said. 'You must have had a blister and it popped. Did you not notice?'

'A bit,' said Josie Smith. 'That's why I couldn't walk so fast.'

'If I'd had a blister like that,' Geoffrey Taylor said, 'I wouldn't have been able to walk at all. You're dead tough, you.'

Josie Smith was pleased about being tough and her little toe didn't hurt any more now it was in the clear water of the stream. But then she looked at her shoe to see if there was a stone in it. There was no stone but there was blood on the white and the shoe was spoiled. She looked at her sock to see if there was a lump or wrinkle in it. There was no lump or wrinkle but there was a patch of blood and the white sock was spoiled.

'What's up?' Geoffrey Taylor asked.

'I'll get shouted at,' said Josie Smith, 'for spoiling my best socks and sandals.'

'No you won't,' Geoffrey Taylor said, 'because it's not your fault. Your mum should have let you put your wellies on to come fishing, and anyway, you can't help it if your feet have grown. My dad's going upstream to fish for trout near where that tree hangs over the water. It's deeper there. We're going to catch tiddlers. Come on, get your net.'

Josie Smith was worried but she got her net and when they started looking for a place where there might be tiddlers she forgot all about her shoes and socks.

'Over here! Over here!' shouted Geoffrey Taylor, crouching down to look at the tiddlers.

'Keep your voices down,' called Geoffrey's dad, upstream fishing for trout.

Geoffrey Taylor was good at finding tiddlers but Josie Smith was better at catching them in her net because she was quieter and more careful. When Geoffrey's dad came to say it was time for their sandwiches, Josie Smith had a lot more tiddlers in her jam-jar than Geoffrey Taylor had in his.

When they were sitting in the grass with their feet in the bubbly water, eating their sandwiches, Josie Smith said, 'Have you caught a fish, Mr Taylor?'

'I'll tell you something you'll not believe,' Mr Taylor said, 'no matter how hard you try.'

'Will I not, Mr Taylor?' asked Josie Smith, screwing up her face and holding her breath, believing as hard as she could. 'I'm believing hard, Mr Taylor. I'm good at believing things.'

'Even fishermen's tales?' asked Geoffrey's dad.

'Yes,' said Josie Smith with her eyes half shut. She didn't know if it was true or not because she didn't know what a fisherman's tail was, or even that fishermen had tails but she'd seen a picture of mermaids in a story book and they had tails.

Geoffrey Taylor's dad put his face near hers and Josie Smith smelled cheese and pickles and he whispered, 'I caught a little silver trout but when I laid it on the bank it turned into a glimmering girl with apple blossom in her hair.'

'Did it, Mr Taylor?' asked Josie Smith, believing hard. 'And what happened to her?'

'She called my name and then she ran away and disappeared into thin air. That's poetry.'

'Is it, Mr Taylor? She didn't come this way, Mr Taylor, or else we would have seen her. We only saw a bumblebee and gnats and a dragonfly.'

'He's having you on,' Geoffrey Taylor said. 'Can we have a drink, Dad?'

They drank the water from Judy's

spout out of the water carrier with its dark green cover. It didn't taste the same as when you put your mouth to the spout in the stone face, but it was very special because of the rough feel of the green cloth.

Then Geoffrey's dad showed them the glittery whirligig beetles flittering in circles on the surface of the water where it was still.

'How can they run on the water?' asked Josie Smith. 'Why don't they fall in?'

'They've got special hairs on their legs to make them into paddle shapes,' Geoffrey Taylor said, 'and they can use them underwater or else on top.'

'And their eyes,' said Geoffrey Taylor's dad, 'are divided in two, so they can see above and below the water at the same time. Now then.'

Josie Smith looked at Mr Taylor and screwed up her face and tried as hard as she could to believe about their eyes being split in two but she couldn't. It was much harder to believe than the little silver trout that turned into a girl. She waited for Geoffrey Taylor to say,

'He's having you on,' but he didn't.

'Is it poetry, Mr Taylor?' she asked.

'Not poetry,' Mr Taylor said, 'science. And that,' he said, looking up and listening, 'is thunder.'

They all looked up at the sky. It was still blue but there were shadows and flashes and angry rumblings all around.

'I can smell the rain,' Geoffrey Taylor said.

'Let's be having you, now,' his dad said. 'We'll have to try and run home before it really starts. Get your shoes and socks on.'

'Josie Smith can't run,' Geoffrey Taylor said. 'She's got a blister and it's burst. Look.'

Geoffrey Taylor's dad looked and said, 'I'll give you a piggy back up the steep and stony part and then you can try and run when we get to Holt's field.'

'Why are we going through Holt's field, Mr Taylor?' asked Josie Smith.

'Because it's thundering and lightning,' Geoffrey Taylor said, 'so we can't go through Tag Wood. Pour your tiddlers back in the water and get a move on.'

'Can't we take them home?' asked Josie Smith. 'And show them to my mum?'

'Don't be daft,' Geoffrey Taylor said, 'they live here. Get a move on!'

A huge crash of thunder came and Josie Smith got a move on, pouring her tiddlers back into their stream and scrambling into her socks and shoes.

Geoffrey Taylor's dad gave Josie Smith a piggy back up the steep and stony path and said, 'Are you frightened of thunder and lightning?'

'No, I'm not,' said Josie Smith,

'and I like getting wet, as well.'

Geoffrey Taylor's dad put Josie Smith down at the stile to climb into Holt's field and said, 'Are you frightened of cows?'

'No, I'm not,' said Josie Smith. Then she thought for a minute and shut her eyes. Then she opened them again. 'I've never touched one, though,' she said.

'Well, you won't be touching them today, either,' Mr Taylor said. 'Look, they're all sitting down because it's going to rain. They won't be bothering about you. Come on!'

They started running across the field towards the road for home. Mr Taylor ran at the front and Geoffrey Taylor behind him. Josie Smith was right at the back, limping and worrying about her shoe.

'It's starting!' shouted Mr Taylor over his shoulder to Geoffrey Taylor. 'Come on!'

'It's starting!' shouted Geoffrey Taylor over his shoulder to Josie Smith. 'Come on!'

'Aher! Aher! Aher!' panted Josie

Smith, limping and worrying about her shoe.

It started. Big fat raindrops splashed on the long grass, sploshed into the buttercups and went splat on Josie Smith's forehead. The cows in the field sat still and got wet and steamed. Why didn't they all go home?

'Mind the carpets!' shouted Mr Taylor over his shoulder to Geoffrey Taylor, 'and hurry up!'

'Mind the carpets!' shouted Geoffrey Taylor over his shoulder to Josie Smith, 'and hurry up!'

'What does he mean? What carpets?' wondered Josie Smith, limping and worrying about her shoe.

'What carpets?' shouted Josie Smith. 'What do you mean, caaaaaaaah!' Splat!

Geoffrey Taylor heard her scream and came running back to see.

'I told you to mind the cowpats!' he said. 'Come on, we're getting soaked!'

When they reached the road home they were soaked. They looked down the steep slope at the rows and rows of houses all the same and the shops and the mills with tall chimneys and everything was dark and soaking wet.

'We might as well not bother running,' said Geoffrey Taylor's dad, 'because we can't get wetter than we are. How's that blister, Josie?'

Josie Smith hid the shoe full of cow muck behind the shoe with the bloodstain and said, 'It hurts a bit.'

'Do you want another donkey ride?' asked Geoffrey Taylor's dad.

'No!' said Josie Smith. She didn't want him to know she'd stood in a cowpat.

'She stood in a cowpat,' Geoffrey Taylor said, 'so you can't carry her now.'

But Mr Taylor opened his rucksack and took out the polythene bag he'd packed their sandwiches in. He made

Josie Smith put her foot in the bag and tied the handles round her leg. Then he gave her a piggy back all the way home in the rain.

Josie Smith dashed in and shouted, 'Mum! I've had a good time and we came home because it rained and there were cows but they didn't touch us! And, Mum, I caught more tiddlers than Geoffrey Taylor and his dad caught a fish that turned into a little girl only we didn't see her because she went the other way and he said fishermen have tails and it's poetry! And, Mum, Geoffrey Taylor said I'm tough because he would have cried if he'd . . . had a . . . blister . . . like mine.'

Josie Smith stopped and looked down at her feet, worrying.

Josie's mum, at her sewing machine, stopped and looked, too.

'Turn round,' said Josie's mum.

Josie Smith turned round.

'And back again,' said Josie's mum.

Josie Smith turned back again. She looked over her shoulder at the back of herself and then she looked down at the front. Josie's mum at the sewing machine was looking, too, and her nose was wrinkled up.

Josie Smith said again, 'We went through Holt's field and there were cows. We had to go that way because it was thundering and lightning . . .'

Josie Smith shut up and stood there. Water from her wet fringe was rolling down her face and water from the rest of her hair was dripping on to her shoulders. The back of her flowered frock was stained with grass and splashed with mud and dirty rain. The front seemed to have more flowers than it had started out with. Sardine coloured flowers and tomato coloured flowers, mostly. Below the frock were wet muddy legs. One leg ended in a squishy dirty shoe with a red patch on it. You couldn't see where the other leg ended because it was inside a polythene bag. You could smell it, though.

'Shall I wash my hands and face?' asked Josie Smith, wondering if she was going to get shouted at.

She didn't get shouted at but she had to wash a lot more than her hands and face. She had to have a bath and have her hair washed. When Josie's mum saw the state her white sandals were in, she stuffed them both in the polythene bag and put them in the dustbin. And still Josie Smith didn't get shouted at.

Josie's mum bathed Josie Smith's sore foot in hot water and disinfectant and put a plaster on it. Then she said, 'I knew you'd get a blister.'

'How did you know?' said Josie Smith. 'You didn't see me change my wellies.'

'No,' said Josie's mum, looking at the clean shiny wellies on the mat by the kitchen door, 'but your wellies are the only things you put away tidily in their proper place. You told me you wanted to look nice for Geoffrey Taylor so why didn't you tell me you wanted to put your sandals on?'

'I don't know,' said Josie Smith. Then she thought for a bit and said, 'Because you always say no. You never let me put them on because they're for best.'

'Not because they're for best,' said Josie's mum, 'because they're too small and I couldn't afford new ones. If they hadn't been peep toes you'd never have got them on at all. And now I'll tell you a bit of news you'll like.'

'Have I to sit on your knee for it?' asked Josie Smith. She only had to sit on her mum's knee if it was really special news.

'Yes,' said Josie's mum, 'come on.'

Josic Smith sat on her mum's knee and listened to the news and smiled. She was going to have some new sandals in time for the garden fête in the park. She told the good news to Percy when she went to bed and she told him a lot of other good things, too. She told him about the glittery whirligig beetles who could run on top of the water but she didn't say they had eyes split in half, even with her eyes shut, because she didn't think he'd believe her.

Last of all, before they went to sleep, she held his woolly head close to hers and told him a story of buttercups and bluebells and the little silver trout that turned into a girl with apple blossom in her hair who ran away and vanished.

'It's all right, Percy,' she whispered, hugging him tight, 'I haven't got my eyes closed. It's poetry.'

JOSIE SMITH'S HOT DAY

'I'm too hot,' said Josie Smith.

'Water your flowers,' said Josie's mum.

'I have watered them,' said Josie Smith. 'My flowers are nice and cool but I'm boiling!'

'Well, water yourself, then,' said Josie's mum. 'Wash your hands and face.'

'I'm not dirty,' said Josie Smith, 'I'm hot.'

'Wash your hands and face,' said Josie's mum, 'and you'll feel better.' And she kept on sewing.

Josie Smith liked the smell of the

flowered cotton stuff that her mum was sewing. She liked the sewing machine noise as well but she was still too hot so she waited a bit and then she said, 'Can I have an ice lolly?'

Josie's mum finished her seam and then she sewed backwards and forwards and backwards and forwards and then she broke the threads.

Josie Smith waited but her mum still didn't say anything. Grown-ups don't like it when you pester, but if they forget what you say to them you have to ask them again.

'Can I have a lolly?' asked Josie Smith.

Josie's mum pulled the flowered stuff out from under the needle and turned it over to look at the back of her sewing.

'Oh no!' said Josie's mum. 'There's something wrong with the tension again!' And big creases came in her forehead. 'If I'm not sick and tired . . .! And what's the matter with you?'

'I want an ice lolly,' whispered Josie Smith, trying hard not to pester, 'I'm too hot.'

'Oh, all right,' said Josie's mum, 'bring my purse. It's on the table.'

Josie Smith brought her mum's purse from the kitchen table. When she came back her mum was pulling at the threads in the seam that was full of knots behind, and the seam disappeared. Josie's mum took the purse and gave her some money and Josie Smith ran out the front door and across to Mrs Chadwick's.

'Hello Josie,' said Mrs Chadwick. 'You look hot.'

'I am hot,' Josie Smith said. 'I'm boiling and I want an ice lolly.'

'Please,' said Mrs Chadwick.

'Please,' said Josie Smith. She had forgotten to say it because she was hot.

Mrs Chadwick's ice lollies were better than the ice lollies at anybody else's shop because Mrs Chadwick made them herself, pouring raspberry red or lemon yellow into little steel tubes in a rack and then putting the sticks in. She had ordinary lollies with paper on them in her fridge as well, but they cost a lot more money and they were flat.

Mrs Chadwick opened the lid of her fridge. 'What colour do you want?' she said.

'Red,' said Josie Smith. 'Please.' With a red one she could play at lipsticks until the top bit had no colour left and was just ice.

Mrs Chadwick gave Josie Smith a red lolly and took her money. 'How's your mum today?' she said.

'The tension's gone wrong,' said Josie Smith, 'and she's got big creases in her forehead.' Josie Smith wasn't sure what the tension was but she knew it always made creases come in her mum's forehead and knots come in her sewing.

'I expect she's got a bit of a headache,' Mrs Chadwick said. 'Now you be a good girl and don't pester.

41

Play outside with Eileen. Off you go.'

Josie Smith went, but she didn't go and call for Eileen next door. She sat down on her own doorstep and put some nice cold lipstick on with her lolly. The doorstep was hot and the pavement was hot and up above the black roofs and chimneys the blue sky waved and wobbled. Josie Smith wanted to know why the sky looked wavy and wobbly but there was nobody to ask. The front door was open behind her back and she could hear the sewing machine going again, so she sat where she was and licked off her raspberry lipstick and put some more on. Melted lolly trickled down her chin and trickled in the collar of her blouse.

She wished Eileen was playing. She wouldn't know why the sky was wobbly but she would be somebody to play with. It was no use calling for her, though. It was Saturday afternoon and, in the morning, Eileen and her mum had been to the hairdresser's. Josie Smith had seen them coming home and smelled the hot perfumy hairdresser's smell that made her wrinkle her nose.

Josie Smith thought going to the hairdresser's was stupid. Josie's mum could cut hair and make curls so Josie Smith never went. Eileen had blonde hair and it was curly. When she went to the hairdresser's it was even curlier and the curls didn't move any more. They were stiff like doll's hair and Eileen didn't play out in case she spoiled them.

Josie Smith finished her lolly and put the stick in her pocket for making things. Then she felt hot again and wondered what to do. She could go up to Mr Scowcroft's allotment and help him pull up weeds and find worms for the hens. Josie Smith liked the hens but it was too hot. She could call for Gary Grimes and play with him but he always wanted to play running about being cowboys and Indians or cops and robbers. Josie Smith liked running but it was too hot. She could run down to her gran's house to see if she was making buns for Saturday tea but then, when she'd eaten her bun, she'd have to run all the way back up the steep street and it was too hot.

Josie Smith got up from the hot doorstep and went inside to her mum.

'What's to do now?' asked Josie's mum.

'I'm still too hot,' said Josie Smith, 'and I'm fed up as well.'

Josie's mum looked at the seam in the flowered stuff. There were knots all along the back again. She banged the stuff down and said, 'Right! That's enough!'

Josie Smith thought she was going to get shouted at but her mum just looked at her and said, 'I'm fed up, as well.'

'Are you too hot like me?' asked Josie Smith.

'No,' said Josie's mum, 'I'm too tired and the sewing machine needs mending. Just look at your face, it's all red.'

'It might be a bit of lolly,' said Josie Smith, touching her cheek and making a black stripe there.

44

'It's not lolly, you're hot. We'd better cool you down. Go and get your bathing costume.'

'What for?' asked Josie Smith.

'Because we're going to have some fun,' said Josie's mum. 'I've got a good idea.'

Josie Smith dashed upstairs and rummaged in her drawers until she found her bubbly blue bathing costume. She pressed its ruffly stuff to her cheek and sniffed its exciting rubbery seaside smell. But they weren't going to the seaside, were they?

Josie Smith dashed to the top of the stairs and shouted, 'Mum? We're not going to the seaside, are we?' But Josie's mum didn't answer. She wasn't in the kitchen. Josie Smith could hear her out in the back yard. She could hear water splashing.

Josie Smith dashed back in her bedroom and opened the window to shout, 'Mum? What are you doing?'

'Put your bathing costume on,' said Josie's mum, 'and come and see.'

Down in the yard below Josie Smith's window there were two big metal tubs. Josie's gran used to say that her mum did the washing in tubs like that but nobody did these days because they had washing machines. The big tubs filled up with rainwater now, and when there was plenty, Josie Smith and Josie's mum got it out with a bucket and washed the big stone flags in the yard. Perhaps that was Josie's mum's idea. It was hard work washing the yard but it was more fun than tension and knots in your sewing, or sitting on the doorstep by yourself. And if you had your bathing costume on you could accidentally splash a bit and get wet.

Josie Smith in her bathing costume ran downstairs and out into the yard. Josie's mum was pouring water into one of the tubs from a white bucket, filling it up because it hadn't been raining.

'Are we going to wash the yard?' asked Josie Smith.

'No,' said Josie's mum, 'but we're going to wash something.'

'Like Gran's mum used to do because she had no washing machine?'

'A bit like that,' said Josie's mum, 'but what we're going to wash wouldn't go in the washing machine, anyway.'

'Why not?' asked Josie Smith. 'Is it too big?'

'Not too big,' said Josie's mum, 'but too wriggly and squeaky.'

'What do you mean?' asked Josie Smith.

'Come here and I'll show you,' said Josie's mum and she lifted Josie Smith up so she could look down into the water. 'I can't see anything in the tub,' said Josie Smith.

'I haven't put anything in there yet,' said Josie's mum.

'But when will you?' asked Josie Smith. 'I want to see the washing that wriggles and squeaks. Mum, go on!'

'Right,' said Josie's mum, and into the tub went Josie Smith. Sploosh!

'Aaaaagheeee!' squeaked Josie Smith, jumping and wriggling in the cold water. 'You've thrown me in!'

'And you do squeak and wriggle a lot, don't you? Are you feet on the bottom?'

'Yes!' squeaked Josie Smith.

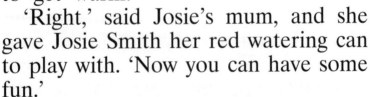

'Are you still too hot?'

'No!' squeaked Josie Smith, jumping up and down to get warm.

'Right,' said Josie's mum, and she gave Josie Smith her red watering can to play with. 'Now you can have some fun.'

'Can I splash?' asked Josie Smith.

48

'You can splash as much as you want,' said Josie's mum. 'Then we just have to sweep the water away afterwards and we'll have washed the yard. Splash away, but be careful not to break your flowers.'

Josie Smith splashed. She held the rim of the tub and kicked. She picked up her feet and sat in the water, floating. She filled her watering can and threw the water frontways towards the wall where the gate was. Splat! She filled it again and threw it sideways to where the kitchen window was. Splat!

'Mum! I'm cleaning the window as well!' shouted Josie Smith.

'Good girl!' shouted Josie's mum. 'I'm making a cup of tea and then I'll come and help you!'

Josie Smith filled her watering can again. She didn't throw any water at the sunny corner where her little garden was with its orange and red and purple flowers. She threw it at the other corner and splashed the shed door.

'Eeow!' screeched an angry voice. It was Ginger sitting on the shed roof.

Ginger didn't like water and he moved away right to the top of the roof and sat there all hunched up in a temper.

'Sorry, Ginger!' shouted Josie Smith. 'But I didn't really splash you, it was only a few drops.'

Ginger stayed hunched up in a temper.

'I won't splash that way again,' shouted Josie Smith. 'Watch this!' And she filled her bucket and threw the water backwards over her head towards the wall of Eileen's yard next door. Splat!

'Eeow!' screamed a voice from behind the wall. Josie Smith stopped splashing. 'Eeow!' screamed the voice again and there was a scrambling of buckets and boxes. Josie Smith bobbed round in her tub and looked at Eileen's wall.

Eileen's curly head appeared. 'Did you throw that water?' Eileen asked.

'Yes,' said Josie Smith.

'Well, I'm telling your mum over you,' Eileen said.

'She said I could throw it,' said Josie Smith.

'Well, I'm telling my mum over you, then,' Eileen said, 'because you've splashed my frock. And, anyway, what are you standing in a tub for?'

'To have a good time,' said Josie Smith, 'and to get cool.'

'That's stupid,' Eileen said.

'It's better than having a bright red face,' said Josie Smith, 'like you've got.'

'I have not got a bright red face!'

'You have!'

'I haven't.'

'You have. Like a red lolly.'

'I'm telling . . .' Eileen started to cry.

'Don't be so soft,' said Josie Smith. 'My face was red as well, but now I'm nice and cool. Ask your mum to let you put your bathing costume on and I'll ask my mum to fill the other tub for you.'

'My mum's gone across to Mrs Chadwick's for some shopping.'

'Ask your dad then.'

'He's having a sleep in his chair.'

'He'll say Yes, then, if you're careful not to wake him up.'

Eileen's head disappeared. Josie Smith sang a song to herself, floating in her tub with her knees tucked up. She turned her face up to the sky and even with her eyes shut tight she could still see golden squiggles of sunshine.

After a few minutes the back gate opened and Eileen came down the steps into the yard in her pink bathing costume and pink plastic sandals and pink and green water wings as well.

'Why didn't you climb over the wall?' Josie Smith asked her.

'Because I don't want to scrape my knees like you're always doing. You always have scabs on your knees.'

'So what?' said Josie Smith. 'It's better than being soft.'

'There's hardly any water in this tub,' said Eileen, peering in, 'and how am I supposed to get in it, anyway?'

'My mum will fill it,' said Josie Smith, 'and then she'll lift you in. Mum!' she shouted. 'Mum! Eileen wants to play!'

So Eileen played as well, squealing and screaming when Josie's mum jumped her into the tub and then holding on to the sides and bobbing about like Josie Smith.

Josie's mum went back to her cup of tea and watched them through the kitchen window.

Then Eileen said, 'I can float without

holding on because I've got water wings.'

'Can I have a go with them?' asked Josie Smith.

'No, you can't because they're mine.'

Josie Smith filled her watering can and threw some water across the yard towards Eileen. Splat!

'Don't you splash me, or I'll tell,' said Eileen.

'I have to splash,' said Josie Smith, 'my mum said. Anyway, I didn't splash you, I only splashed near you.' She filled her watering can and threw some more water. Splat! This time it went a bit nearer and hit Eileen's tub. Then she stopped. Josie Smith in her tub looked across the yard at Eileen. Eileen in her tub looked across the yard at Josie Smith. They didn't say anything for a long time.

'You'd better not splash my curls,' Eileen warned her, looking worried.

Josie Smith filled her watering can.

Eileen crouched down in her tub but her curls still showed over the top. 'It's not fair, anyway!' she wailed. 'I've got nothing to splash with!'

Josie Smith waited, holding her full watering can with both hands.

Eileen said in a very small voice, 'It's not fair.'

'You can splash with your hands,' said Josie Smith, but she knew it wasn't fair so she shouted, 'Mum! Can Eileen have something to splash with?'

Josie's mum brought a plastic jug from the kitchen but Eileen started crying.

'It's not a watering can!' she wailed. 'I want the red watering can.'

'Let her have a go,' said Josie's mum, 'and don't be selfish.'

'She's got water wings she can play with.'

'You can't splash with water wings,' Eileen said. 'That's stupid! I don't want to play with them!' She pulled off the water wings and threw them out on to the ground. 'You play with the water wings. I want the red watering can!'

Josie's mum picked the water wings up and put them on Josie Smith and winked. Then she gave the plastic jug to Josie Smith and the red watering can to Eileen and said, 'Let me get out of the way before you start.'

She got out of the way and they started.

'You haven't to splash my curls, though!' Eileen shouted. 'Or I'm not playing.'

'And you haven't to splash my flowers!' Josie Smith shouted, 'or I want my watering can back!'

They splashed and splatted and squealed and shouted and jumped and bobbed and wriggled and shrieked until there was hardly any water left in their tubs and Josie Smith didn't splash

Eileen's curls and Eileen didn't splash
the flowers.

Josie's mum came out and washed
the windows with a sudsy sponge.

'There's hardly any water left,' said
Josie Smith. 'Can we have some more?'

'In a minute,' said Josie's mum.
'Remember I put you in that washing
tub to be washed.' She went in and
came out again with soap and a bottle
of shampoo. She started washing Josie
Smith. Josie Smith, covered in
soapsuds and with her soapy hair

shaped into a pointed pixie hat, shouted, 'Sing the bubble song, Mum! Go on, sing!'

So Josie's mum sang, 'I'm Forever Blowing Bubbles...' And Josie Smith and Eileen sang, too, but only Josie Smith had bubbles in her tub.

'I don't want to be washed,' Eileen said, 'because I'm clean already.' Eileen was always clean. 'And I don't want my hair washing, either, because that's clean as well.'

'How will we get the soap off my hair?' asked Josie Smith. 'With the plastic jug?' And she looked across at Eileen who still had the watering can. She really wanted her hair rinsing with her red watering can but Eileen was holding it very tight.

'Wait and see,' said Josie's mum, 'I've got a better idea.' She went inside and came out again with the big white bucket and a colander.

She gave the colander to Josie Smith and Eileen watched, holding the watering can tight.

'What have I got to do with it?' asked Josie Smith.

'Hold it over your head,' said Josie's mum. 'No! Not like that! It's not a hat. Hold it the right way up and as high as you can. And keep your eyes shut so the soap doesn't go in.' Josie Smith held the colander as high as she could and kept her eyes shut.

'I've got my eyes shut!' she shouted. 'But, Mum, what are you going to—'

Sploosh! A cold shower came down on Josie Smith's head.

'Argh! Mum! Mum! You've . . . argh!' Josie Smith started to laugh. She laughed so hard that she couldn't stand up and had to hold on to the tub. Her mum was laughing just as hard because Josie's face had almost disappeared under her streaming wet hair.

Eileen watched, clutching the watering can hard.

'Again!' shouted Josie Smith. 'Go on, Mum, do it again!'

Josie's mum went to fill her bucket and Josie Smith jumped and splashed and giggled with her wet hair heavy on her face.

Josie Smith heard Eileen say, 'I want a shower like Josie Smith.'

But Eileen couldn't have a shower. Eileen had forgotten her curls.

Josie Smith opened her eyes but she couldn't see anything through her wet hair. She pushed the hair away and looked across at Eileen in her tub. Eileen was holding the colander high up over her head and she had her eyes shut. Josie's mum was lifting the bucket.

'No!' shouted Josie Smith. 'Mum, don't—'

Down came the cold shower on Eileen's golden curls and the curls unrolled and streamed down over Eileen's face. Eileen laughed and giggled. Josie's mum laughed, too. Josie Smith didn't laugh. She stood in her tub, holding the rim, and waited for Eileen to remember.

Eileen remembered.

'Aaaaaaaaah!' she screamed. 'Aaaaaaaah! Aaaaaaaaaaaah! My curls!'

'You haven't got any curls,' said Josie's mum, 'not now.'

Eileen screamed and wailed and howled and cried. You couldn't see her tears because water was still streaming down from her hair, but her face was all red and creased up.

'Aaaaaaaaah!' she screamed. 'Aaaaaaaaah!'

'What's to do with her?' shouted Josie's mum above the screaming noise. 'It'll dry.'

'She's been to the hairdresser's,' shouted Josie Smith. Then she shouted, 'Eileen! Shut up! If your mum comes back she'll be able to hear you from the kitchen and she'll look over the wall and then you've had it!'

Eileen shut up.

'That's better,' said Josie's mum. 'Now then, out you get, both of you and we'll get Eileen's hair dry.'

Josie's mum lifted them both out and then she rubbed Eileen's hair with a towel and combed it. Sometimes, it hurts to have your hair combed when it's wet and tangled but Josie's mum started at the bottom so it hardly hurt at all and Eileen was so scared of her mum finding out that she kept quiet. She was really still crying but you could hardly hear her. Sometimes you could hear a little wailing noise, 'Mmmmmmm . . .' And sometimes a little sniffy noise of 'Nf, nf, nf.'

62

Josie's mum brought out a kitchen chair and sat Eileen in the sunniest patch in the yard, near Josie Smith's flowers.

'Your hair will be dry in five minutes,' she said. 'Don't worry.'

Eileen sat in her chair in the sun while Josie's mum polished the kitchen window with a wash leather and Josie Smith put her wellingtons on and washed the yard with a big sweeping brush and the sudsy water from her tub. Every so often Eileen went, 'Mmmmmmm...' and every so often, 'Nf.' By the time they had finished, Eileen's hair was dry.

'Is it dry?' asked Eileen.

'Yes, it is,' said Josie Smith, 'only...'

'It's dry, all right,' said Josie's mum, 'but...'

Eileen stopped crying and smiled. Then she felt her hair.

'Aaaaaaaaah!' she screamed. 'My curls have gone! You've made my curls go! My hair's straight! Aaaaaaaaaah!'

'Oh, no,' said Josie Smith.

'Oh dear,' said Josie's mum. And they stood there staring at Eileen's hair. You couldn't exactly say it was straight but it certainly wasn't curly. It hung down in yellow tails that were a bit frizzly and wriggly at the bottom.

'What's happened to Eileen's curls?' whispered Josie Smith.

'It's a perm,' whispered Josie's mum.

'What's a perm?' asked Josie Smith.

'A permanent wave,' said Josie's mum. 'The hairdresser puts some special stuff on your hair and heats it up and it curls your hair and it stays curly for a long time.'

'My mum said I haven't to tell!' wailed Eileen.

Josie Smith wasn't listening to Eileen. She wanted to know all about the perm.

'Does it smell horrible?' she asked.

'It does a bit,' said Josie's mum.

Josie Smith remembered the nasty hot perfumy smell when Eileen came home from the hairdresser's.

'She's had a perm, then,' said Josie Smith, 'so why is her hair not curly?'

'Because your mum wet it!' screamed Eileen. 'If you wet it you have to put rollers in!'

'That's stupid,' Josie Smith said, 'if you have a perm and you have to put rollers in as well.'

'It is not stupid!' screamed Eileen, 'because it stays curly all the time until you wash it again and you've got to put rollers in for me now and some lacquer on it or else my mum'll find out and then you've had it!'

Josie's mum looked at Josie Smith and Josie Smith looked at her mum. They didn't have any lacquer. They didn't have any rollers, either.

'We'd better go in,' said Josie's mum, 'and see what we can do.'

They all went in and Eileen sat down on a chair in Josie Smith's front room.

'You bring the hairdryer down,' said Josie's mum, 'and I'll go and get the lacquer.' And she winked.

Josie Smith brought the hairdryer down and sat and watched her mum.

Josie's mum dipped her comb into a plastic bowl of water and combed a bit of Eileen's hair, winding it round and round her finger and drying it with the hairdryer. She did Josie Smith's fringe like that when Josie Smith wanted it curly. It made nice curls but they didn't come out stiff like Eileen's. What would happen when Eileen found out there wasn't any lacquer? Her mum must have been telling a little lie when she said she'd go and get some because when she said it she winked.

When Josie's mum had finished and Eileen had curls all over her head, Josie Smith held her breath.

'Now you have to spray it,' Eileen said, 'like the hairdresser always does.'

'Right,' said Josie's mum. 'You shut your eyes.'

Josie Smith watched Eileen shut her eyes. Then she watched her mum lift her hand up with nothing in it at all and press her finger on nothing at all and say, 'Sssssssss! Sssssssss! Sssssssss! There. You're done.'

66

'I didn't feel anything,' Eileen said.

'You're not meant to,' said Josie's mum. 'I did it very carefully.'

'I didn't smell anything, either,' Eileen said.

'I know,' said Josie's mum, 'because the lacquer I use is magic lacquer and it doesn't smell. Do you want to look at yourself?'

Josie Smith looked worried. If Eileen looked at her curls she might touch them, too.

'Yes I do want to look,' said Eileen, 'because my curls have got to be the same as before or else I'll get in trouble.'

Josie Smith looked very worried.

Josie's mum lifted Eileen up and showed her the curls in the mirror.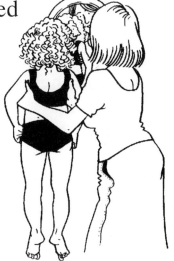

'They're nearly the same,' said Eileen, 'but—'

Josie Smith held her breath.

'But what?' said Josie's mum.

'But nicer,' Eileen said, and she lifted her hand up to feel.

Josie Smith closed her eyes.

'And they're nice and stiff,' said Eileen. 'Now I'm getting my water wings and going home.'

'Wait!' shouted Josie Smith, jumping up. 'Eileen, wait!'

'What do you want?' said Eileen.

'To touch your curls,' said Josie Smith. 'Can I touch them, just a bit?'

'All right, you can if you want,' said Eileen, 'but you'd better be really careful and not spoil them or your mum'll have to do them again.'

Josie Smith was careful. With just one finger she touched one curl and the curl was as stiff as doll's hair. She touched another and then another and they were all as stiff as doll's hair. Eileen took her water wings and went home.

'Mum,' said Josie Smith as soon as Eileen had gone, 'can I have a curl in my fringe for the fête tomorrow?'

'All right,' said Josie's mum.

'With magic lacquer, as well?' asked

Josie Smith.

'You wouldn't like your hair to be as stiff as a doll's,' said Josie's mum.

'No I wouldn't,' said Josie Smith, 'but I like the magic lacquer.'

'Then I'll tell you a secret,' said Josie's mum. 'You're good at keeping secrets, aren't you.'

'Yes,' said Josie Smith, 'really good.'

'Well, see that you keep this one,' said Josie's mum, and she whispered in Josie Smith's ear, 'I melted sugar in the water I used to curl Eileen's hair and that's why it dried all stiff.'

Josie Smith smiled and she said, 'I'll have my curls made with ordinary water, then. So when you spray the magic lacquer on they'll stay all nice and soft.'

'That's a very good idea,' said Josie's mum, 'and I'll do the same with mine. But we'd better do it tomorrow. Remember we haven't had a perm like Eileen so our curls won't last so long. And that's another secret.' She put a finger on Josie Smith's lips. 'We mustn't tell anybody about Eileen's curls not being natural. That would be nasty. Promise.'

'I won't tell,' said Josie Smith, 'I promise.'

So, the next day, when Josie Smith and Eileen were playing out and they started quarrelling, Eileen said, like she always said, 'And anyway, I'm better than you because I've got curly hair!' Josie Smith opened her mouth and shut it again. She didn't want to spoil it for Eileen because Eileen was her best friend.

Josie Smith at the Garden Fête

On Saturday morning, the day of the garden fête, Josie Smith woke up really early. It was so early that there were no morning noises. So early that the house was still asleep. But it was morning. Josie Smith knew it was morning because when she sniffed she could smell the morning outside her window and light was coming through the curtains. It was nearly as exciting as Christmas and when it's as exciting as that it means that it will be ages and ages and ages before you're allowed to get up.

Josie Smith got up, anyway. She slipped out of bed very quietly and

71

tucked Percy Panda in because he was still warm and sleepy. She peeped at her new blue sandals, wrapped in tissue paper, still in their box, ready for this afternoon. Then she got behind the curtains and sat down on the windowsill to look out at the day.

It was only just light. It was still a bit dark down in the back yard, and behind that, the slate roofs of all the houses were very black and quiet. Row after row after row of them, all the way up the slope, all black and quiet and still asleep. Up behind the last row was the hill with a tower on top and up above that was a pale pink, pearly sky. Higher up, the sky was sleepier and a few stars were still lit. Butterflies fluttered inside Josie Smith's tummy. She saw Ginger walking along the wall of the yard. In summer, if the weather was fine, Ginger played out all night. Josie Smith opened the window.

'Ginger! Ginger! Come in! I want to tell you about the garden fête.'

When Ginger heard her voice he jumped off the wall to wait at the kitchen door.

Josie Smith crept downstairs to let him in and then she gave him some breakfast.

'Josie!' shouted Josie's mum from her bedroom. 'What are you doing up at this time?'

'Nothing!' shouted Josie Smith.

'Get back to bed!' shouted Josie's mum. 'Or you'll not go to the fête!'

Josie Smith got back to bed but she was too excited to get back to sleep. Instead she hugged Percy's big warm head next to hers and sniffed his fur and whispered all the things she could remember from the posters that were in the windows of the shops.

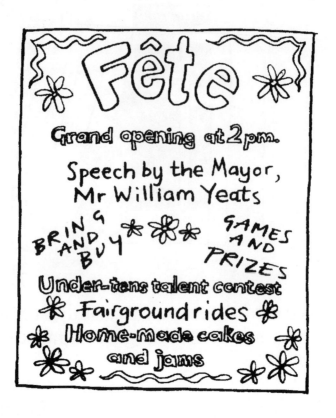

Fête

Grand opening at 2 pm.

Speech by the Mayor,
Mr William Yeats

BRING
AND
BUY * *** GAMES
AND
PRIZES

Under-tens talent contest
* Fairground rides *
* Home-made cakes *
and jams

'And I'm going to wear my new blue sandals, Ginger. I wish you could come but there's no prize for the best cat. And I wish it was time to get up.'

But it wasn't.

'Ginger? D'you want me to tell you the poem that Geoffrey Taylor's dad told me yesterday? He made it up once when we went fishing and I can say it, as well, now. It starts off with: *I went out to the hazel wood . . .*'

74

Josie Smith told Ginger all about the little silver trout that turned into a girl. She didn't get stuck once, not even when she came to the hardest bit that was about the hollow lands and hilly lands. When the poem was finished Josie Smith and Percy fell asleep again and when they woke up it was really morning and breakfast time.

Josie Smith sat on the doorstep all morning, crayoning. The sunshine came to warm her head but Eileen didn't come out to play.

Eileen went to the hairdresser's with her mum and when they came back, with their hair all stiff and perfumy, Eileen's mum said, 'Our Eileen's got to practise her song for the talent contest.' And they went in.

Josie Smith got up from the warm doorstep and went in the house where it was cool.

'Mum? Eileen's going in for the talent contest so can I go in for it, as well?'

Josie's mum, mashing potatoes, said, 'You can if you want.'

'But what will I do?' asked Josie

Smith. 'I'm not so good at singing.'

'Do a dance then,' said Josie's mum. 'Something Miss Pendlebury's taught you at dancing class.'

'They're not proper dances,' Josie Smith said, 'they're positions and bending your knees and pointing your toes. I can't do that.'

'Wash your hands and face,' said Josie's mum. 'Your dinner's ready. You don't want to be late setting off, do you?'

Josie Smith washed her hands and face and tried to eat her dinner, but the butterflies in her tummy wouldn't let her and, when her mum wasn't looking, she gave her meat to Ginger under the table.

Afterwards, Josie Smith had a bath with some of her mum's bubbles in the water and then she put on a clean vest and knickers and new white socks to go with her new blue shoes.

'Mum, am I really wearing my best frock today?'

'Yes,' said Josie's mum, 'and see that you don't rip it. I'm not making you another this year.'

76

Josie Smith's best frock was white muslin flocked with tiny red and blue velvet squares and it had a thin blue velvet ribbon for a belt with a little bow and a press-stud. When her mum put the frock over her head the soft flocked muslin made her feel tingly all over  because she liked it so much and she closed her eyes and sniffed its clean and special smell as it came down over her face.

Her mum said, 'Put your cardigan on.'

'Oh, mum!'

'Put your cardigan on or you'll have that frock filthy before we even get to the park. And you'll look well going in for a talent contest, standing on the stage with ice-cream all down your front.'

'Will there really be a stage?' asked Josie Smith while her mum buttoned the navy blue cardigan right up to keep her clean.

'I expect so. Why don't you do the dance you learnt for the school concert? We can take your ballet shoes. They'll go with the red squares on your frock.'

'My ballet shoes! We'll take my ballet shoes!'

'Quieten down,' said Josie's mum. 'Now, listen to me. Are you sure you want to wear your new sandals? Because if you do there's to be no climbing trees, no playing football with Gary Grimes and Rawley Baxter and no walking on the grass. It'll still be soaking wet after that storm the other day.'

'But where can I walk, then?' asked Josie Smith. 'It's all grass in the park.'

'You stay on the path with me and your gran and Eileen's mum and dad and Eileen.'

Josie Smith made creases in her forehead, thinking. She thought about the new blue sandals, all smooth and clean inside. She thought about staying on the path with Eileen when everybody else was playing on the grass. She thought about her friendly wellingtons and felt the tiny velvet flocks on her skirt. Then she decided.

'I'll go in my wellies,' she said, 'and have a good time and play on the grass. And when it's the talent contest I'll take my cardigan off and my wellies and put my ballet shoes on.'

The new blue sandals stayed in their box in tissue paper and Josie Smith and her mum set off to the park. Eileen and her mum and dad were setting off at the same time. Josie Smith stopped in front of the house next door to look at Eileen's frock. It was pale pink like the morning sky and made of funny bubbly stuff that reminded Josie Smith of a bathing costume.

'It's new, my frock,' said Eileen. 'Yours is not.'

Josie Smith opened her mouth. She was going to say, 'Well, I've got new shoes on, so Ner Ner Ner!' But she shut her mouth again without saying it because she remembered she hadn't got them on. Then she said, 'I've got my best frock on.'

'It's not new, though,' Eileen said, 'it's old. I've seen it hundreds of times.'

'You have not.'

'I have.'

'Oh no you haven't because my mum doesn't let me wear it hundreds of times because it's for best.'

'Well? Who cares, anyway? It's a horrible spotty frock. It looks like it's got measles.'

They all set off down the street and Josie's gran was waiting at the bottom to go with them.

Everybody else was walking down to the park, too. Gary Grimes and Rawley Baxter and Rawley Baxter's little sister and Jimmy Earnshaw pushing his two-wheeler bike and Geoffrey Taylor and his dad and all the children from Albert Street.

They went down the main road to the traffic lights and then all the way down the steep slope to the station and then along the lane beside the railway lines, past the empty mills with frightening chimneys, until they came

80

to the park.

A glittery band was playing with a big drum going Bam! Bam! Bam! There was red, white and blue bunting fluttering in the summer breeze and a cool smell of grass and a hot smell of toffee apples. There were blue and yellow swing boats and people shouting and sawdust and stalls with cakes and homemade jam and balloons and bouncing toys on sticks and a great big tent and a field for races. Josie Smith was so excited that she could hardly breathe and her chest hurt and inside her she could hear the big drum. Bam! Bam! Bam!

As soon as they were in the park, Eileen's mum said to Eileen, 'Now remember what I told you. Don't start!'

Eileen started: 'Can I have some ice-cream? Can I have a go on the swing boats? Can I have a toffee apple? Can I have a balloon? Can I have—'

'What have I told you about pestering?' shouted Eileen's mum. Then she gave her some money and Eileen bought loads of things and one was a balloon with ears.

'Mum...' said Josie Smith very quietly.

'Don't you start,' said Josie's mum. Josie Smith didn't start. She didn't want so many things as Eileen but she would have liked a balloon. She didn't want one with ears. She thought they were babyish. But there were silver balloons and gold balloons and she'd never seen those before. They shone in the sunlight and Josie Smith stayed behind to look.

'Here you are, love. I can see which ones you fancy.' The balloon man held out the strings of a gold and a silver balloon. 'Which one's it to be?'

Josie Smith took a deep breath and said in a very small voice, 'No thank you.'

The balloon man turned away and sold a balloon with ears to a lady with a baby in a pram. The lady tied the balloon to the pram handle, and the baby looked up at it, pointing.

'Josie? Josie!' Josie Smith had got left behind. Her gran came back to get her. 'We don't want you getting lost,' she said, 'do we, now?'

'No,' said Josie Smith.

'What's to do with you?' asked Josie's gran.

'Nothing,' said Josie Smith, looking up at the beautiful gold and silver balloons shining in the blue sky.

'Well, you run on, then, and catch your mum up or she'll think you're lost. Go on. I can't run at my age. I'll walk behind you.'

Josie Smith ran to catch up with her mum and Eileen was still pestering: 'Can I have that china dog? Can I have that pink T-shirt? Can I have another ice-cream?'

When Josie's gran caught up with them, she said, 'You're not upset, are you?'

And Josie Smith said, 'No.'

'Well, that's good,' said Josie's gran. 'Did you have your eyes shut when you said that?'

'Yes,' said Josie Smith.

'You don't want all that rubbish Eileen's bought, do you?'

'No,' said Josie Smith with her eyes half shut.

'Whisper to me,' said Josie's gran, 'and tell me what you'd really like. It's not pestering, you know, if I've asked you.'

Josie's gran bent down and Josie Smith whispered. 'A balloon.'

'No!' said Josie's gran. 'I don't believe it! What? A pink balloon with ears like Eileen bought?'

'No,' said Josie Smith, still whispering. She made creases in her forehead to look serious as she explained, 'A silver one . . .'

'Oh,' said Josie's gran, 'a silver one. Well those are nice. Of course the gold ones are very nice, too. I nearly bought one myself but an old lady like me can't be going around with a balloon. What would people think?'

'I could carry it for you,' said Josie Smith, looking hard at her gran, 'and then give it to you when we get home.'

'That's an idea,' said Josie's gran, 'and then when I go to bed tonight I can tie it on the end of the bedstead so I'll see it as soon as I wake up tomorrow morning. D'you think that's a good idea?'

'Yes,' said Josie Smith, looking worried, 'but the balloon man's a long way back now and they cost a lot of money as well.'

Josie's gran said to Josie's mum, 'We'll catch you up in a minute. I just want Josie to help me with something.'

'Do you want me to run back and get you a balloon, Gran?' asked Josie Smith.

'Well, if you say they cost a lot of money . . . I was wondering if we should have a look in my magic handbag. Shall we?'

'All right,' said Josie Smith, watching all the children running towards the swingboats and waving silver balloons. There were probably no more left. 'But . . .'

'You don't think there'll be anything? We've always found something before.'

'I know.' Usually it was toffees. Once

there were some flags for sandcastles at the seaside. But flags were small. A balloon wouldn't fit in a handbag, even a magic handbag. But Josie Smith didn't want to upset her gran so she felt around inside the bag with her eyes shut while her gran held it open.

'What can you feel?' asked Josie's gran.

'Your purse,' said Josie Smith, 'and your face powder and your keys.'

'Is that all? Is there nothing else?'

'No,' said Josie Smith, 'there's nothing, except for a bit of string.'

'String? No, no,' said Josie's gran, 'I don't put string in my handbag. What would I want string for?'

'I don't know,' said Josie Smith, 'but Gary Grimes always has string in his pockets and I don't know what he wants it for.'

'Well, pull it out and give it to Gary Grimes. I don't want string in my best magic handbag.'

Josie Smith started pulling. She pulled and pulled and said, 'I can't find the other end of it.'

'Well it must be somewhere,' said Josie's gran, 'because you can't have a piece of string with only one end to it.

Keep pulling!' Everybody who came past stopped to laugh at Josie Smith pulling and pulling out the piece of string.

'Gran, it goes up your sleeve to the back of your cardigan!' Josie Smith ran round behind her gran and there was the other end of the piece of string. There was a silver balloon tied to it and it had been following them all the time. Everybody laughed and Josie's gran said, 'What did I tell you? An old lady like me carrying a balloon! You see how everybody's laughing.'

'I'll carry it for you, Gran,' said Josie Smith, and they walked on to catch up with the others.

When Eileen saw the silver balloon she started:

'I want a silver balloon like Josie Smith's!' And when her mum said No because she already had a balloon, Eileen burst it and stamped on it and her mum gave her some money for a silver one.

'Let's go!' yelled Geoffrey Taylor who was fed up with Eileen. 'Races!'

And he ran off across the
grass. Jimmy Earnshaw
and Gary Grimes and
Rawley Baxter and
Rawley Baxter's little
sister and Josie Smith
ran after him across the wet
grass that was drying in the
sunshine.

Rawley Baxter's little sister
held the silver balloon while Josie
Smith and Geoffrey Taylor won the
three-legged race and got a red
toffee apple each. Josie Smith got
some red toffee on her face and
when she tried to get it off she got
a bit on the sleeve
of her cardigan.
But when she
looked down
at her best
frock it
was still all
lovely and
clean.

90

Afterwards, Josie Smith tied the silver balloon to a rhododendron bush and they did a tug-of-war and Josie Smith's side lost. On the side that won, all the children from Albert Street fell down in the mud, each one knocking down the next one like a row of dominoes. Josie Smith's side got pulled forward and they all went tottering through a big patch of mud.

'Aaaagh!' screamed Josie Smith, trying not to fall. Then she tripped up and fell. Splat!

'Aaaagh!' yelled Jimmy Earnshaw who was in front. Josie Smith had knocked him over. It was Jimmy Earnshaw who had gone splat and Josie Smith had landed on top of him and Gary Grimes had landed on top of Josie

91

Smith and everybody else had landed on Gary Grimes except for Rawley Baxter's little sister who was right at the end and let go. Gary Grimes started crying.

'Shut up, Grimesy!' ordered Jimmy Earnshaw and Gary Grimes cried louder.

'Don't be so soft,' said Josie Smith. Then she looked down at her best frock. It was still clean.

After the races they were hot and thirsty and Geoffrey Taylor's dad bought them all an ice-cream cornet, a really big one in two different colours. The ice-cream melted in the sunshine faster than you could eat it. Some trickled down inside the sleeve of Josie Smith's cardigan and a pink blob flopped off the top of the cone and fell but, luckily, most of it slid down inside her wellington and when she looked down at her best frock it was still clean.

'Let's have a wrestling match,' Gary Grimes said.

'I'm not,' Josie Smith said, 'because I have to keep my frock clean. I'm going in for the talent contest with Eileen.'

'I am as well, then,' Gary Grimes said, because he always copied everything that Josie Smith did. Then somebody shouted, 'Hide and Seek and Gary Grimes is on!' So, they played Hide and Seek and Josie Smith hid so well in the rhododendron bush that Gary Grimes never found her and she had to come out by herself because they'd started playing Tig.

Then, on top of the noise of the band, they heard an announcement:

'Will all children wishing to take part in the talent contest please come to the tea tent.'

Josie Smith ran off towards the big tent and Gary Grimes ran after her.

When she got there she was hot and out of breath.

'Aher! Aher! Aher!' she said. Then she remembered—the silver balloon! She ran all the way back and found the silver balloon still tied to the rhododendron bush. Nobody had pinched it. She ran even harder back to the tent. Aher! Aher! Aher!

A very tall man said, 'Give your names to the lady at that table.'

There were some dahlias in a vase on the table and it wasn't a lady, it was Jimmy Earnshaw's mum. She wrote Josie Smith's name on a piece of paper and said, 'What are you going to do for us, Josie? Are you going to sing like Eileen?'

'No,' said Josie Smith, 'I'm not so good at singing. I'm going to do a ballet dance.'

'That's nice,' said Mrs Earnshaw, 'and have you brought some music with you?'

'Yes . . .' said Josie Smith, hoping she could still remember it.

'Give it to me, then,' Mrs Earnshaw said.

Josie Smith stared at her and wondered what to say. How could she give the music to Mrs Earnshaw when it was in her head?

'I have to count to three,' she said, looking very hard at Mrs Earnshaw, explaining, 'because two other fairies go on before me and there's a fairy queen but she's asleep and we tiptoe round her and sprinkle magic dust and it's glitter.'

94

'All right, love,' Mrs Earnshaw said, 'I'll tell the pianist to play something nice for you. D'you want to leave your balloon with me?'

'Yes please,' said Josie Smith. 'It's my gran's balloon and I have to look after it for her.'

'It'll be safe with me,' Mrs Earnshaw said, and she tied it to her chair.

Then Josie Smith looked all round and saw a long table at one side of the tent where there was tea and cake and ladies talking and sitting down and her gran was there and Mrs Chadwick from the corner shop. In the middle some people were standing up and at the other side was a little stage. On the stage was another table at one side with a vase of dahlias and two men and two ladies sitting at it. Next along sat a man with white hair wearing a big fancy chain. Josie Smith knew he must be Mr William Yeats, the mayor, whose name she had learned from the posters, because she'd seen a chain like that in a story called Dick Whittington, Lord Mayor of London. On the near side of the stage, where there were steps up, there was a piano. There wasn't a pianist, though. Mrs Ormerod from the baby class at Josie Smith's school was playing it. The tent smelled hot and sweaty and grassy.

The tall man went up the steps and walked to the front of the stage.

'And now, ladies and gentlemen, Eileen is going to sing for us I'm Forever Blowing Bubbles, a song my mother used to sing to me and which I'm sure you all remember.'

Everybody clapped and Mrs Ormerod started playing.

Eileen, in her new bubbly dress, walked on to the stage and stood at the front.

Eileen knew all the words and sang them really loud and sometimes she held her skirt out and sometimes she pretended to blow bubbles up at the sky and sometimes she twirled round and round.

Josie Smith, watching, thought Eileen was fantastic.

Then something happened that was really fantastic. Eileen sang the song all over again and, this time, when she pretended to blow bubbles, real bubbles came floating all around her like magic. Josie Smith held her breath and stared. She stared at Eileen's bubbly dress that was as pink and pearly as the morning sky, and at Eileen's perfect yellow curls  and the floating bouncing bubbles all around her, pink and blue and green and glistening.

Even Gary Grimes was staring.

'It's dead good that,' he said, 'with them bubbles.'

'I know it is,' Josie Smith said, 'and Eileen's my best friend.'

Everybody clapped and Josie Smith clapped louder than anybody.

Rawley Baxter came up to them, pushing and shoving, and said, 'Eileen's mum blew them bubbles. You could see her shoes under that screen over there.'

'Well?' Josie Smith said. 'What's it got to do with you, anyway? Eileen's my best friend.' And Rawley Baxter went away.

Josie Smith was supposed to be next but she was still staring at the bursting bubbles and Gary Grimes pushed past her. He climbed up on the stage, walked to the front and stopped. Mrs Ormerod played two big chords—Da-der!—and waited. Gary Grimes just stood there. Mrs Ormerod played the chords again, louder—Da-der!—and then she looked round to see what he was doing. Gary Grimes just stood there.

Next to where Josie Smith was waiting, Mrs Earnshaw looked at the paper with their names on it.

'He said he was going to juggle,' she said.

Gary Grimes just stood there.

Josie Smith wondered how Gary Grimes was going to juggle if he didn't have anything to juggle with. He did feel in his pockets for a minute and Josie Smith wondered if he was going to juggle with the dirty bits of string and broken Dinky cars and toffee papers he always kept in them but he didn't. He just stood there.

Mrs Ormerod look across at Mrs Earnshaw and Josie Smith saw her lips say, 'What shall I do?'

'Play something and we'll get him off,' Mrs Earnshaw said in a loud whisper. But the minute Mrs Ormerod started playing, Gary Grimes roared out at the top of his voice: 'Jugglin'!'

Then he burst into tears and his mother came and lifted him down and carried him away, still roaring.

'Go on, Josie,' Mrs Earnshaw said, 'it's your turn.'

Josie Smith started climbing the steps. A voice shouted, 'Josie! Josie, wait!'

'Miss Josie Smith will now do a ballet dance for us.'

Everybody clapped but the voice shouted again, 'Josie!' It was Josie's mum. Josie Smith couldn't see her but she heard her and remembered. On the top step she stopped.

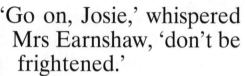

'Go on, Josie,' whispered Mrs Earnshaw, 'don't be frightened.'

But Josie Smith stood there on the top step, stuck fast like Gary Grimes. She didn't want to be like Gary Grimes who didn't juggle but she couldn't do her dance in her dirty cardigan and she was frightened of turning round and going back down the steps when Mrs Earnshaw was telling her to go on. She felt her face go red and a lump got stuck in her throat and made some tears squeeze out of her eyes. She didn't want to be a cry baby like Gary Grimes who didn't juggle.

Then Mrs Earnshaw's voice whispered in her ear, 'What's the matter, love?'

'I've got to take my cardigan off,' said Josie Smith. 'It was only to keep my frock clean and I can't do my dance in it.'

'Well, take it off, then,' Mrs Earnshaw said. 'Here, turn round and I'll help you.'

Josie Smith turned round and Mrs Earnshaw helped with all the buttons that went right up to her neck.

'Right. Off you go.'

Mrs Ormerod had got fed up waiting and was already playing some music. It wasn't Josie's Smith's music so Josie Smith hummed the right music to herself and counted to three and set off to the front of the stage on tiptoes. It was very slippery. Josie Smith wondered why it was slippery because Eileen hadn't slipped and Gary Grimes hadn't slipped when they went on. But there was no time to think so much about the slipperiness. Josie Smith, at the front of the stage, held out her pretty muslin skirt and pointed her toe.

Everybody started laughing. They laughed and laughed and laughed and a boy from Albert Street shouted out, 'What are you supposed to be? A ballet-dancing hippopotamus covered in mud?'

Josie Smith stood there, as stuck as Gary Grimes who didn't juggle, and her chest went Bam! Bam! Bam! like the big drum. She had remembered something else. They had played Hide and Seek and Tig and she didn't think she had looked at her frock afterwards. Another tear spilled over as Josie Smith held her breath and looked very carefully down her front.

Her frock was clean.

It was all right. Josie Smith humming and pointing her toe, smiled at everybody.

They laughed. They laughed and laughed and laughed as if they couldn't stop.

Somebody said, 'What a little comic!' and people held on to each other and got out handkerchiefs to dry tears of laughter from their eyes.

Josie Smith stared down at all the laughing faces and then she saw something. At the back of the tent where the tea table was, a hand, Josie's mum's hand, was holding something up. Somthing red. Josie Smith's red ballet shoes.

Josie Smith, stuck like Gary Grimes who didn't juggle, looked back over her shoulder. There was a trail of slippery mud prints all the way back to the steps. Then she looked down her front past her clean frock to where she was pointing her toe. Her wellingtons were covered in sloshy, brown mud and one was decorated with a pink splash of ice-cream and the other with a pink rhododendron flower.

The music played and the people laughed and the children from Albert Street shouted.

'Eh! You've got toffee apple all over your nose!'

'She's toffee-nosed!'

'Except you can't see it for the dirt!'

'Cry baby! Cry baby!'

'I am not!' shouted Josie Smith, losing her temper. 'I am not a cry baby!'

The music stopped playing and the people stopped laughing and the children from Albert Street stopped shouting.

Everything went quiet. Josie Smith took a deep breath and thought for a minute and then began in a very small voice that got a bit bigger as she went along:

'I went out to the hazel wood . . .'

She had told Percy the poem this morning so she knew she could say it all, and when she got to her favourite bit where the little silver trout turned into a girl, she spoke up as much as she could:

'It had become a glimmering girl
With apple blossom in her hair
Who called me by my name and ran
And faded through the brightening
air . . .'

She did her very best, but without Percy's woolly head to snuggle to, she got a bit stuck at the hardest part.

'Though I am old . . .'

What was it? Oh, what was the bit about hollow lands and hilly lands?

'Though I am old . . .'

She couldn't remember it. Somebody, thinking the poem was finished, started clapping and then stopped.

'Though I am old . . .'

Then a man's voice spoke very very quietly behind her, helping:

'Though I am old with wandering
Through hollow lands and hilly
* lands . . .'*

Josie Smith, remembering, spoke up:

'I will find out where she has gone
And kiss her lips and take her hands
And walk among long dappled grass

And pluck till time and times are done
The silver apples of the moon,
The golden apples of the sun.'

Everybody clapped and clapped and Geoffrey Taylor's dad pushed through all the people till he got to the front and lifted Josie Smith down from the stage. Mrs Earnshaw brought her the silver balloon and said, 'Well done.'

Josie Smith heard Eileen's mum say, 'If our Eileen doesn't win there'll be trouble.'

Eileen won and went on the stage again to be clapped.

'You did very well, too,' Mr Taylor said to Josie Smith. 'You got stuck for a bit but you picked up nicely. I think you deserve a treat What's it to be?'

'A ride on the swing boats with Eileen!'

So they had a ride on the swingboats with their heads hanging back to look at the swinging treetops in the blue sky. Their silver balloons rode above them.

After that they had some cake and Josie's mum pulled Josie Smith's toffee nose and said, 'I'll give you ballet shoes!

I've been carrying these things round all afternoon! And do you know who it was who helped you with your poem?'

'No,' said Josie Smith. 'It must have been magic. It wasn't Geoffrey Taylor's dad because he was a long way away out at the front and nobody else knows the poem except him and me.'

'Well, I know who it was because he came and told me,' said Josie's mum. 'It was the Mayor.'

'The Lord Mayor of London?' asked

Josie Smith.

'No,' said Josie's mum, 'our Mayor. Come with me. He wants to say Hello to you.'

The Mayor wasn't up on the stage any more. He was sitting with the ordinary people having a cup of tea.

'Will you shake hands with an old man, Josie?' he asked.

Josie Smith shook his hand. She thought he must be a hundred years old at least but he was nice and quiet and had white whiskers growing on his ears.

'You brought a tear to my eye, do you know that, Josie?'

'No,' said Josie Smith, and then she said, 'I'm sorry.' He didn't look as if he'd been crying. His face was crinkly with smiles like Father Christmas.

'Can you tell me who wrote that lovely Song of Wandering Aengus, Josie?'

'Nobody did,' said Josie Smith. 'Geoffrey Taylor's dad made it up when he was fishing and he told it to me. He wasn't having me on. And it's not a song,' she explained, as politely as

108

she could, 'it's poetry.'

'It is indeed,' said the Mayor, 'and it was written by a man from Ireland and I was named after him. Have you been crying a little yourself, Josie?'

'No,' said Josie Smith with her eyes shut tight because it was a lie. When she opened them she saw the Mayor wink at her mum and then they went away.

'Mum,' said Josie Smith, 'why do grown ups screw their eyes up without shutting them for big lies and wink one eye shut for little ones?'

'I don't really know,' said Josie's mum.

When the last of the tea had gone cold and the cake was all eaten and the jam was all sold and the stalls were bare and the swingboats empty, everybody started going home. They didn't go so fast because it was uphill and they were all tired. Josie Smith and

Eileen walked together, swinging their arms and waving their silver balloons and singing I'm Forever Blowing Bubbles till their throats were sore. The boys all walked together, pushing and shoving and calling each other names, and Gary Grimes was sick.

'He's had five ice-creams,' his mother said, 'I warned him this would happen.'

When they got to Josie's gran's, Josie Smith gave her the silver balloon and her gran said, 'You know, I think you should take it home for Percy. I bet he'd like to have a silver balloon at the end of the bed. It'd keep him company when you're out playing.'

Josie Smith was really tired and when she was washed and in bed she could still feel the sun burning her face and smell it on the skin of her arms, though the evening was as cool as her sheets.

'Look at your balloon, Percy,' she whispered in his fluffy black ear. 'I bet we'll be able to see it shining even when it goes really really dark. I've got hundreds of things to tell you about the fête . . .'

She thought she was telling him but perhaps she was dreaming. She could see the green grass and red white and blue bunting and the glitter of the band and Eileen's bubbles. She was swinging up and down and looking at the sky and the sky was full of balloons and the trees were covered with gold and silver apples.

'Percy . . .' she whispered, wanting to wake up and tell him. 'Percy . . .' but Percy was warm and too fast asleep and so was Josie Smith.